JURASSIC GIRL

JURASSIC GIRL

THE ADVENTURES OF MARY ANNING
Paleontologist and the First Female Fossil Hunter

Michele C. Hollow

ULYSSES BOOKS
FOR YOUNG READERS

Published by:
Ulysses Books for Young Readers,
an imprint of Ulysses Press
PO Box 3440
Berkeley, CA 94703
www.ulyssespress.com

ISBN: 978-1-64604-717-8
Library of Congress Control Number: 2024934558

Printed in the United States
10 9 8 7 6 5 4 3 2 1

Front cover design: David Hastings

IMPORTANT NOTE TO READERS: Although the author and publisher have made every effort to ensure that the information in this book was correct at press time, the author and publisher do not assume and hereby disclaim any liability to any party for any loss, damage, or disruption caused by errors or omissions, whether such errors or omissions result from negligence, accident, or any other cause.

For Steven, the funniest man I know.
Thank you for so much joy and laughter.

INTRODUCTION

As a journalist, I spend a lot of time researching facts. I love nonfiction, especially when it covers people doing amazing things. That's Mary, an exceptional person who lived in the early 1800s.

In conducting my research for this book, I connected with Richard Wells, a historian at the Lyme Regis Museum in Lyme Regis, UK. He answered a number of my questions about Mary's interest in fossils, about her education, her family, and the day-to-day activities in her hometown. I read biographies and novels about Mary, including *The Fossil Hunter* by Shelley Emling and *Remarkable Creatures* by Tracy Chevalier.

Not everything in this story is factual. I made up all of the conversations. Obviously, no one from Mary's time period can verify what Mary and others in this story said. Looking at Mary's life and imagining her interactions with those around her, I hope you gain a glimpse into a remarkable individual.

I also created a couple of characters to connect to the main ones. I filled in parts from incomplete histories. The whole process was like putting a puzzle together.

The more I learned about Mary, the more I respected her. Mary's ability to keep going despite challenges and hardships made me believe she was an optimist with a strong and determined personality.

I hope you'll love her as much as I do.

—Michele C. Hollow

CHAPTER 1

MARY'S BOOTS SUNK INTO the mud and the hem of her long dress clung to her legs. Something caught her eye. She reached into the shallow water, shook off the seaweed, and pulled out an unearthly object. It resembled the other fossils in her basket, except this one had an almost complete claw, which poked through the stone. Seeing the claw, Mary imagined a strange beast covered in scales, crawling along the rocks behind her. She envisioned a time when odd creatures roamed the earth.

Since the age of five, Mary had been collecting, scraping, and polishing the fossils she found. Now twelve, Mary handled knives, chisels, picks, and small hammers with precision. Her father, who was fossil-hunting nearby, would have given her his sharp tools sooner, but her mother hadn't allowed it.

She filled her basket with fossils and instinctively watched for signs of impending lightning. Today was quiet; few tourists strolled the beach. A well-dressed boy about her own age approached. Judging from his clothes, she guessed he hailed from London.

He watched her dig in the mud. Fingers laced with seaweed, she held what appeared to be a small rock. She swished it back and forth in the seawater to wash off the slime and tangled mess. Satisfied, she placed it into her basket.

The boy shouted over the waves as they noisily crashed into the rocks. "What are you doing?"

"Working," she answered.

"On what?"

Mary continued digging. When she glanced up again, she could see the boy was still looking at her, waiting for an answer. "I'm hunting for treasure," she said.

"Pirate treasure?"

"There are no pirates in Lyme Regis."

"Then what?"

"Fossils. The beach in Lyme Regis is the best place to find them," Mary said, showing him what she had found. "All kinds of strange creatures lived here in the sea and on the land."

"How odd," he said, studying the fossils.

"They provide clues to our past," Mary said.

"You're not like most girls."

"Why? Because I'm not pretty and proper?"

"No—you're pretty," he stammered. "It's just that, well, you're not girly."

"Because I don't run when a small fish swims by or shriek when my hands are covered in goo?" Mary laughed.

"That's not what I meant . . . or maybe I did."

"That's okay, I'm used to hearing that," she said. "But fossils are amazing. Let me show you. That is, if you don't mind getting your fancy pants dirty."

The boy huffed at Mary's insult before rolling up his trousers, lacing his shoes together, and swinging them over his shoulder. Soon, mud covered his feet. He was entranced as he watched Mary seemingly pull fossils out of nowhere. He tried to imitate her but came up empty-handed.

A boy several years younger let go of his father's hand and raced over to watch. Mary noticed that he was freckled, with reddish blond hair like the older boy's.

The boy raised his voice, "Who's your friend?"

"I'm Mary. Mary Anning."

"Well, my name is David," the younger boy announced.

"I'm Neil," the older boy said. "And this is my brother."

"What are you looking for?" David asked.

"Fossils," Mary and Neil said together.

"Can I see?" David asked.

Mary rummaged through her basket and found something to show David.

"This is a belemnite fossil I found earlier this morning," Mary said. "It gets its name from a Greek word meaning 'spear.' See how it looks like a little dart? People used to think they were darts thrown down to earth during a thunderstorm."

Both boys listened eagerly.

"It's also called the 'Devil's Finger,'" Mary added.

"Ooh, that's scary," David said.

"Look closely. You can almost see his fingernail. And the ruddy color." Mary winked at Neil, adding, "Looks like dried blood."

"Ooh . . . can I hold it?"

Mary placed the Devil's Finger in David's hand. He examined the fossil carefully.

"But what is it, really?" he asked.

"It's the remains of an ancient sea creature, most likely," Mary said. "Maybe a small fish or squid-like thing."

"I can see that," Neil said. "Look at its shape."

"Exactly," Mary said.

"Are they real?" David asked.

"Of course they are," Neil said, staring at Mary for reassurance.

She smiled back at him, knowing he trusted her.

After combing the seaside for a couple of hours searching for more fossils, the boys' father called out to them. "It's getting late!"

"I wish we had more time," Neil said. "You found so many, Mary. Fossils are not so easy to spot."

David agreed. "Some rocks look like they may contain a fossil inside," David said. "I'm trying to figure out the difference between an ordinary rock and one with a hidden fossil."

"One way to tell is by touch," Mary said. "See how smooth the surface of this fossil is?"

"Yes," David replied.

"Rocks have a rougher finish," Mary explained. "And fossils often stand out because their colors differ from ordinary rocks. The colors of the rocks are more uniform."

"Thanks, Mary," David said. "I'm going to ask Father if we could buy one." He ran to his dad and grabbed his hand, pulling him toward Mary.

"Hello. My son tells me you sell seashells," the boys' father said.

"They're fossils," Neil corrected him.

"I'd like a Devil's Finger," David said. "It's a belemnite."

"I'd like this one," Neil said. "You can see the tail of a fish."

"A pence for both?" the boys' father asked.

"Six pence," Mary answered.

"Six pence!" the boy's dad replied. "Two pence for the both of them?"

"Six pence for the two," Mary said. "They're unusual."

"They're small."

"And one of a kind," Mary said.

"Three pence for the two."

"Well, I haven't polished them—five pence it is," Mary said.

"Five? I said three." He waited for Mary to respond. "Well?"

The ferry bell rang. The father reluctantly pulled the five pence out of his pocket and handed it to Mary.

They walked to the dock, their father in front with Neil and David trailing behind. Neil turned to Mary. "I'm going to look this up when I get home," he said and, head down, he plowed toward his father. Little David looked back at Mary and gave her a broad smile.

Mary was pleased with herself. Another sale made, and another fossil skeptic converted to a believer.

CHAPTER 2

MARY'S STOMACH RUMBLED. SHE had been at the seaside with her father since early morning, and now the sun was starting to set. Her father had filled up a large sack with stones that contained the hardened remains of clams, snails, slugs, and octopus parts.

As they walked, the wind began to pick up and a loud cracking sound caught their attention. Mary and her father looked up as a slab of rock fell from the cliffs into the sea. Rocks more than 200 million years old stemmed from below the ocean and rose several stories high on parts of Lyme Regis. Another large rock loosened from the cliffs and plummeted into the ocean, splashing them.

"Lightning!" her father exclaimed over the sounds of the ocean. "We'd better go before it rains."

Mary's father took his scarf and put it around his daughter's neck. "The wind is getting stronger, and I can see rain over the ocean in the distance."

Mary smiled as her father took her hand in his, and she quickened her pace. Water covered the tops of her boots, and the waves grew stronger and closer. They washed over the sand and rocks.

Mary looked back to see what the waves left exposed. More Devil's Fingers and a handful of trinkets covered in debris were scattered upon the shore. She pulled her father's hand, leading him back toward the ocean.

"No, Mary, we'll come back tomorrow when the tide's out. Pretty soon, the waves will be taller than you." Although he knew it was dangerous, he admired his daughter's courage. While he occasionally took risks when he was by himself, with Mary present, his rule was to avoid hazardous weather conditions at all costs. He would never expose Mary to danger.

As they headed up the dirt road to their home, Mary took large steps to keep up with her father, who moved at a rapid speed with his long, lean legs. Hearing Mary's heavy breaths behind him, he slowed his pace so she could catch up and walk beside him.

***

Richard Anning was a cabinetmaker, but he spent most of his time searching the shores of Lyme Regis with his daughter. Usually, Mary's older brother, Joseph, and their dog, Tray, whose long black and white coat was often dusted with sand, joined them.

They had all the tools they needed to carefully chip away at the hardened sediments surrounding the small prizes inside the rocks. Richard taught Mary what to look for and how to polish her finds. Sometimes a fossil stuck out from inside a rock or the remains or impression of an animal or plant became part of the rock. Those were easy finds.

Richard gave Mary a small rock hammer to break away sediment on the fossil. He taught her not to use too much force to keep the fossil intact.

For fossils that hid inside rocks, she used a small chisel to scrape and pry the fossil free.

Mary didn't keep most of what she found, selling even the prettiest of the fossils. The colorful ones usually sold for triple the amount of the plain ones. All of the fossils varied in shape, size, and markings. Odd in appearance, they were sure to be of interest to someone—especially those who'd never seen anything like them before.

The day before, Mary had found a three-foot-long ammonite, called a "snake stone," a fossil of an extinct animal that had a coiled, snail-like shell. She'd also found a foot-long piece of shale with half a dozen or so fish skeletons embedded into it. The fossilized fish formed a pattern on the slab of shale. They looked as if they were swimming upstream.

Mary had worked alone. Her father had been at the shop behind their house, building a chair for a new customer. So, she'd lugged the pieces home. They weren't too heavy, just awkwardly large; when she placed the fossils on their sides, they came up to her hips. She'd tried her best to keep them from dragging on the ground as she carried them. A scratch or break would have made her finds less valuable. She knew they'd fetch a fine sum because both pieces were so unusual. With every find, she felt as if someone had left her a gift.

Today, her load was lighter and she had her father by her side. The Annings lived about a quarter of a mile from the shore, far from the hotel and fine houses located farther up the hill. Tourists from London visited Lyme Regis for the quiet and fossils.

***

MARY AND HER FATHER turned up the dirt road onto the steep narrow street where they lived. At first, Mary didn't see the large rat gnawing on a bone with hardly any meat left on it. Her father shuddered, which made her look. When she spotted the brown rodent, she wished Tray was by her side. His shrill bark sent the feral animals scurrying away. While Mary loved most animals, she hated the rats because they were more brazen than the wild hogs. Both came out at night, when people were indoors, to feast upon the trash. Occasionally, a rat wandered outside in the middle of the day.

Their two-story cottage with bay windows on both sides of the front door had enough room for Mary, her brother, her parents, and Tray. They didn't need much. Mary loved the view from her bedroom window. From there, she could see the ocean, smell the salt air, and hear the waves as they crashed onto the rocks. When it stormed, however, the waters reached all the way into their home's first floor.

Mary and Joseph shared a bedroom right above the living room. Richard had built a wall dividing the room to give his children some privacy. Mary got the space with the window. She had to pass though Joseph's room to get into hers.

Richard and Molly's bedroom was also on the second floor. Each bedroom had a basin for washing and a broom with a dustpan to sweep up the sand Mary often brought with her after spending a day on the beach fossil-hunting. The kitchen was the largest room in the house. With no formal dining room, the Annings placed the table Richard made in the kitchen. It was next to the living room, which would soon become the Annings' Fossil and Furniture Shop.

The Annings planned to turn the front room into a fossil shop. Tourist season was a few months away, a perfect time to sell fossils to visitors.

***

Mary held up the hem of her dress so as not to leave a trail of sand on the clean wooden floors. She washed up, changed out of her sandy clothes, and went to help her mum with dinner. Molly dished out the boiled oatmeal and topped it with pats of butter. She was in an unusually good mood because Joseph sold the two fossils Mary had found the day before to a tourist visiting the beach. It meant a few pieces of mutton in tonight's porridge.

"You should have seen her, Molly," Richard said. "A tourist wanted to give our Mary one pence for two fossils. She wouldn't have it. She got five. You would have been proud of her."

Mary smiled at her father and handed her mum the coins. They clinked when Molly deposited them in the glass jar that she kept in the cupboard. Molly was in charge of the money; she had put half away from yesterday's sale to cover one month's rent. Together, the fossils had sold for four pounds, leaving her with enough money to buy breakfast, lunch, and dinner for almost two weeks.

Mary set the table with the wooden spoons and bowls her father made, while Joseph stirred the beer on the stove. The family drank beer because the water wasn't safe to drink and the alcohol content in the beer was minimal.

Richard was almost finished with the display cases for their new shop, which would soon open. Mary suggested naming it "Fossils and Furniture," even though Richard hadn't sold any furniture for a good part of a year. He had a new customer who'd ordered a chair, which made Molly incredibly happy because it fetched a high price. Given the choice, however, he preferred to spend time fossil-hunting with his children than in his shop making furniture.

"Joseph, move that fossil off the table so we can eat supper," Molly said.

Molly pulled the freshly baked bread out of the oven, and its aroma filled the room. Mary's mouth watered thinking about how good dinner would taste. She tore the warm bread into bite-sized pieces and dropped them into her oatmeal.

As Richard sliced into the bread, crumbs from the crust fell onto the wooden table. "You do such good work," Molly said. "It's a shame more people know you as a fossil hunter than a cabinetmaker. Each time Mary and I set the table, I'm reminded of how hard you worked on this. It's the nicest piece of furniture we own."

"The chair I'm making is much fancier."

"We're not fancy," Molly replied.

"Mum's right," Joseph said.

"Well, I am." Mary got up, bowed, and curtsied. "And Papa, we'll place two of your chairs in the front room next to the fossils so tourists can try them out."

"And maybe I can cushion the chairs," Joseph said. "Mr. Stevens agreed to take me on as an apprentice. I start tomorrow. He welcomed me into his textiles shop and factory. He has three daughters around my age. I think he'll be a fair boss since he has children. I know the factories in London take terrible advantage of children: long hours, little pay, and no rest. Some children as young as six work in those factories. Mr. Stevens wanted to know my age. He doesn't hire small children. He seems principled."

"Joseph, I'm so proud of you."

"Yes, I know, Mum."

"Joseph, do you really want to be an upholsterer?" Richard asked, almost whispering so as not to disappoint his wife. "I thought you prefer fossil-hunting."

"Papa, we need to eat. I'm fifteen and ready to work. Mr. Stevens will teach me the trade and pay for my meals while I learn. I can help you and Mary dig for fossils on Sundays, my day off."

"You take after your mother. Responsible."

"Have to be," Molly said. "You and Mary take too many risks. It's a wonder you've never been hit by falling rocks, lost your footing, or been swept out to sea."

"You worry too much, m'dear. Mary and I are careful."

"No. You and Mary can be reckless at times. Your focus is on the hunt, not what's around you. I don't want to lose another child."

Richard got up and hugged his wife while Mary and Joseph ate their supper. Molly had given birth to ten children. Joseph was the first who'd survived. The seven before him had died in childbirth. A year after Joseph was born, Molly gave birth to a daughter she named "Mary," who died in a fire at their home when she was a toddler. Two years later, she gave birth to another girl, the Mary who'd grow up to love fossil-hunting. This Mary had been a sickly child with frequent fevers and colds, until lightning struck her, miraculously curing her of the frequent illnesses. Richard recalled how he'd called her his "little thunderbolt."

Mary believed lightning helped her predict a change in the weather. Even when there wasn't a cloud in the sky, she felt the coming tempest in her bones right before the weather went from sunny to stormy.

CHAPTER 3

THE MORNING SUN FILLED Mary's room, waking her. Outside her window, she could hear seagulls circling overhead in the cloudless sky. When she was little, she used to fret about them getting swept away by the rains, until her father explained they take cover before a storm. Today was a great day for spending time on the beach. Unlike yesterday, there wasn't a cloud in the sky, making it the perfect day to hunt for fossils.

She filled a basin with water to wash her face and hands, then inspected the dress she had worn the day before. It was a plain ankle-length dress in forest-green, Mary's favorite color. Her mum had made it for her. The hem was still damp, and a bit of sand remained. She opened the window and flapped the dress against the outside wall; the sand disappeared into the sea below. Mary closed the window. It faced the ocean, and during violent storms when the rain came down in buckets and the sea rose, water seeped inside.

Satisfied, she put on her dress, laced up her boots, and placed her basket on a bench by the front door.

Joseph woke at 6 a.m. He needed to report to Mr. Stevens's shop promptly at 7 a.m. Richard had gotten up early to see his son off for his first day of apprenticeship. That morning, he'd given Joseph a small hammer passed down to him from his father, who also worked as a cabinetmaker. Richard had used it when he learned his trade. It was still in good shape, despite numerous scratches on the handle.

Molly was up, too. She used the stove to toast a few pieces of bread from last night's dinner, then smothered it with jam before giving it to Joseph, who was about to head outside for his first day of work.

Mary wandered into the kitchen and sat down beside her father. "Want to come to the beach with me?"

"Your papa has to finish the chair," Molly said, answering for her husband.

"Looks like you're on your own," Richard said. "If I finish early, I'll join you at the seaside."

"Ooh yes, Papa."

"Don't encourage him." Molly was concerned that Richard wasn't spending enough time on completing the chairs.

Molly walked over to Mary and pulled a long piece of ribbon from her apron pocket to tie around her daughter's thick, brown hair, which was a bit unruly. Several wavy strands strayed. Molly did her best to pull it back in a long ponytail. "Wear your bonnet," she said. "It'll keep the hair from your eyes."

Mary ate the last two pieces of toast, which she covered with the jam her mother had made. She finished a cup of strong-brewed tea. "I'll be back with fossils," she yelled, as she adjusted the green bonnet and headed out the door.

Tray scampered out after her. "Glad you're here," she said, petting him. "You're good company."

Tray wagged his tail and trotted alongside Mary down the hill to the seaside. Sometimes Tray sped up his pace, wandered a few paces ahead, and then returned to be by Mary's side.

Mary and Tray had the beach to themselves. Like most days, today was quiet; the locals gathered on the beach to cast fishing lines in hopes of catching dinner. They nodded to one another while they focused on their catch, and Mary turned her attention to finding fossils.

The tide was out, giving her and Tray room to explore. She combed the beach, hoping to find something unusual. She separated ordinary rocks from fossils. From time to time, the fossils were as hard as rocks and often looked a lot like them. The different shapes, patterns, textures, and colors provided clues.

Her father had taught her that plant fossils tended to be darker than the rocks that washed up on the beach, and single-cell animal fossils were lighter in color. This difference was one way to separate the two. Texture was another. Her father had said, "Bones are porous, and animal fossils look a bit like a sponge." She ran her fingers over a dozen fossils. Sometimes, the plant fossils revealed leaf patterns.

She had an easier time with the animal fossils, especially the odd-shaped ones. Occasionally, a beak, skull bone, scale, tooth, or claw peaked out from the object in her hand, making it easy to identify.

The sun stood high in the sky, and it grew warmer. Someone laughed. Mary looked around and saw a stranger rubbing Tray's tummy. He rolled in the sand, enjoying the attention.

The girl was well dressed, like the tourists who came to Lyme Regis on holiday. Next to her were two baskets. One contained fossils.

"Hello," Mary said, then introduced herself. "I see you've met Tray. Glad he's not bothering you."

"Not at all. I'm Elizabeth Philpot. You're lucky you have such a good dog."

"Tray's great company." Mary bent down to pet him and brush the sand off his coat. "He and I spend a lot of time here. I see you collect fossils, too."

"I do,' " Elizabeth said. She was perfectly groomed, sure of herself, and mature. She seemed to be seven or eight years older than Mary. "Fossils provide clues to our past."

"Yes!" Mary almost shouted. "I was telling someone that yesterday. You know about fossils?"

"I do," Elizabeth answered.

Mary beamed.

"How nice to meet someone who appreciates fossils as much as I do," Elizabeth said. She carefully looked at the fossils in Mary's basket, examining each one.

"Look at the pattern on this one," Elizabeth said, holding it up to the sun.

"Looks like a snake," Mary said. "Tourists call them snake and viper stones."

"I know, but it's only a piece of him," Elizabeth said. "You can tell from the break that he was much longer. I'd love to locate the rest of him. Where'd you find him?"

"Over there," Mary said, pointing. "I can show you."

They walked over to the area by the rocks and water. "It's ankle deep," Mary said. "You'll get wet and ruin your boots."

"I don't care, especially if we find something unusual," Elizabeth said.

They filled up their baskets with more Devil's Fingers and snake stones. Each time Mary picked up a snake stone, she studied the edge to see if it was a match. Her stomach grumbled.

"Oh, where are my manners?" Elizabeth said. She had heard Mary's stomach grumble. "Would you like to share some of my lunch? My sister—her name's Mary, too—packed two sandwiches for me because she knows I spend hours and hours out here."

"That's very kind," Mary said, taking the sandwich. It contained beef, a rare treat for Mary.

Elizabeth tore a piece from her sandwich to give to Tray.

"You're going to spoil him!" Mary exclaimed. "He doesn't eat that well at home."

"He's such a good dog," Elizabeth said.

"The best," Mary said hugging him. "I've never seen you here before. Are you visiting?"

"No. My brother arranged for me and my sisters, Mary and Margaret, to move here a few weeks ago. We're in the cottage up the hill. I was eager to get to the beach, but I needed to help them get settled or you would have seen me sooner. We lived in the heart of London, far from the beach. Being here's better because I can go fossil-hunting whenever I want."

"London?" Mary said. "Lyme Regis is a big change from London."

"Yes. Ever been?"

"No. I've only lived here."

"I prefer the quiet here, not too many people. And the fossils. Have you been collecting them long?"

"Yes," Mary said. "I want to learn more about them."

"Come to my house. I get the London Geological Society's newsletters. They're filled with all sorts of information about fossils."

"Oh, I'd like that."

"Not too many girls share your enthusiasm," Elizabeth said. "My sisters and I haven't been here too long. What I've observed is that you're the only girl on the beach fossil-hunting. And all the fossil hunters are men. The London Geological Society doesn't allow women in their ranks; even their newsletters never mention finds from women. It's all men's accomplishments."

"True. Girls around here gossip about boys, don't care about fossils, and hate getting sand in their boots. I don't attend school. My family can't afford to send me. I go to Sunday school. Reverend Wheaton believes in science. You very well might find him here on the beach searching for fossils."

"Most of the girls in my Sunday school have zero interest in fossil-hunting. I love the hunt. I love the find. I'd rather do this than attend a social event or talk about the latest crush. This is definitely more fun."

"Mary, I should be getting back. My sisters will want my help at home."

"I should be going, too. My house isn't far from here. You'll pass it on the way."

"Elizabeth, do you go to school?"

"My parents hired a governess to teach my sisters and me. My brother went. Did you learn about fossils in Sunday school?"

"A bit. As I mentioned, Reverend Wheaton loves science and religion. He believes in both. He's brought fossils to class, and while he's talked about them, I got most of my fossil knowledge from my father."

"Well, he taught you well."

"My papa has a lot of tools. He showed me what to look for, how to use tools, and how to polish my finds. He even tried to teach me to be patient when I'm chipping away so I don't break anything. That's hard sometimes. I've been doing this since I was five."

"Since you were five? Wow. How old are you?"

"Twelve."

"You must own lots of fossils."

"No. I rarely keep them. The other day, I found a spiral-shaped fossil with bright flecks of red and green on it. It even sparkled when I held it up to the sun. It was an ammonite, an ancient marine animal. Papa attached a light metal loop on one end. We sold it for three pence. My brother, Joseph, and I often sell our finds on the beach to tourists. We're opening a shop in our home. You should come by."

"I'd love to. I can stop by on my way to the beach in the morning. Then we can go hunting for fossils."

"We're almost at my house. It's right over there."

"You're close to the ocean."

"Yes. I have a wonderful view from my bedroom window. Sure you don't want to come in?"

"Not today. I need to help my sisters. I'll stop by in the morning."

"I'm usually out by eight," Mary said.

"Me too. I like getting up when the sun's out. See you then."

CHAPTER 4

ONCE HOME, MARY PRACTICALLY skipped through the door. Her parents sat around the dinner table, talking. Joseph wasn't home yet, and Molly worried. She put dinner on hold until her son was back, so everyone could eat together.

"I made a friend," Mary announced. "She loves hunting for fossils almost as much as I do. She invited me to her house so I could look at her collections and read her books. And she has newsletters from the London Geological Society. She said I could read them. She even shared her lunch with me and Tray."

"Slow down," Richard said. "She fed Tray?"

"Yes. Tray and I ate beef sandwiches."

"He'll not want to eat our food," Richard said, petting him.

The dog wagged his tail, happy to receive the attention. He placed his paws on Richard's lap and stretched out his neck while Richard continued to pet him under his chin. Tray sat down and Richard brushed his hands together to remove the sand, which now covered his hands from Tray's fur.

"She fed Tray?" Molly asked, preoccupied. "She must be well off."

"Yes. What's wrong, Mum?"

"She's worried about your brother. He's not home yet." Turning his attention to Molly, Richard added, "He should be walking in the door any minute. You'll see."

"He left before seven," Molly said.

"I know. I was here," Richard said.

The Annings were pleased that Joseph didn't work in a London factory where most children and adults labored fourteen or more hours each day with no breaks. Wages were poor and factory workers had no sick time or days off. If you didn't show up, you lost your job.

"It's almost seven now," Molly said, just as the knob on the front door turned. It was Joseph. He looked exhausted.

"How was your day?" Richard asked.

"Fine and long—very long."

"Well, tonight, Mary and I'll set the table and wait on you," Molly said. "Tell us about your day. Did Mr. Stevens treat you well? What did you do? Did you make anything? Did Mr. Stevens feed you?" She was anxious to know how her son had fared on his first day.

"Slow down, Molly, m'dear," Richard said. "Mary, please bring dinner to the table while I try to calm your mother."

"Yes, Papa."

Mary spooned the porridge into large bowls and brought them to the table, while Molly pulled up a chair for Joseph. Mary stirred the beer brewing on the stove and filled four large glasses.

Joseph tried his best to answer his mum's questions. He wasn't much of a talker, and at the moment, keeping his eyes open took some effort. Molly, however, asked about every detail. He started with what he had for lunch.

"Mr. Stevens gave us oatcakes with boiled milk and treacle, which were really good. He showed us the tools and taught us how to measure enough fabric to cover a chair. He said we must be careful not to waste any fabric; he uses the scraps to make quilts. It's not hard. I'll get better doing it over and over again."

"How many of you did he bring on?" Richard asked.

"Five. James Mann started today."

"He's a good boy," Molly said. "I know his mum."

"We walked home together, and he told me how lucky we are to have this apprenticeship. His cousin, Brian, works in a textiles factory in London. He's twelve and he's on the factory floor at six in the morning and gets home around nine at night."

"It's criminal how they treat children," Richard said. "Those big factories are the worst. They exploit children. It makes me angry."

"Mr. Stevens is kind," Molly said. "Some children as young as six years old work in textiles factories in London and other big and small cities. Mr. Stevens, maybe because he's a father, doesn't take on children so young. And he treats them well."

"Well, he runs a small shop and it's not as bad here as in the big city," Richard said.

"James told me Brian and a lot of children eat watered-down porridge with onions and oatcakes for breakfast and lunch, and oatcakes with milk and treacle for dinner."

"I heard the children and adults eat standing at their workstations," Richard said.

"That's what James said. If they sit, they may fall asleep and their bosses would fire them. I'm thankful Mr. Stevens is a patient man. One of the apprentices cut the fabric wrong. Mr. Stevens took him aside and showed him what to do. He didn't yell or sack him. There are fewer people here than in London. However, Mr. Stevens didn't have to hire any of us. I think he believes he can teach us this trade. I'm fortunate he's kind.

"Today wasn't bad," Joseph continued. "I've a lot to learn and there are much worse jobs. I might like this. Who knows, in a few months, I might get a full time position working for Mr. Stevens."

"We can go fossil-hunting on Sunday," Richard said.

"That would be nice, but not too early. I need to sleep late on my day off. I'm glad today is Thursday. I'm easing into the work week."

"Good night," Molly said, hugging her son. She was thrilled Joseph had a good job with a responsible boss, more responsible than Richard. Fossil-hunting didn't pay the bills as well as textile work. The pay, while not great, was steady and could be counted on.

Mary cleared the table and Molly washed the bowls, spoons, and glasses. They put them in the cabinets Richard had made. Mary turned to her parents and yawned. "I'm going to bed. My friend Elizabeth and I are going to the beach tomorrow if it doesn't rain."

"Invite her in," Molly said. "I'd like to meet another girl who likes fossils as much as you do!"

"I will! Good night." Mary hugged her parents and went off to bed. She looked forward to introducing her new friend to her family.

CHAPTER 5

Mary moved the covers over her face to block out the sun. Tray jumped up on her bed and pulled them back with his teeth. The clock on her wall let her know that Elizabeth would be knocking on her door in half an hour.

She got up, washed her face, got dressed, and went into the kitchen. By then, her parents had already eaten. Joseph had left an hour before, and Richard was in his shop, almost finished with the chair.

While Mary drank her tea, she heard a knock at the door.

"Must be your friend," Molly said. "Invite her in for a cup of tea."

Molly put a fresh pot of tea on the stove, and Mary showed Elizabeth the remaining fossils in her collection. The Annings' living room, or front room, housed all of the fossils Mary, her brother, and father collected.

Mary opened a drawer in a cabinet her father made; it revealed a few dozen reddish-beige rocks; many resembled squid parts. All had multiple arms, and the ones that weren't broken had inward-curving hooks at the end.

"Do you know what these are?" Mary asked.

"I do. I read about them in the latest edition of the London Geological Society's newsletter. You should come by and read it. You can order a subscription."

"I can't," Mary said. "Any money I make helps my family."

"I'll tell you what, I'll share my newsletters with you." Elizabeth was eager to help Mary. She looked around and could see few furnishings and not much else. She knew a number of the geologists in London and thought she'd introduce Mary to them.

What impressed her was Mary's determination. Yes, Mary knew a lot about fossils, and she was smart. However, her eagerness to learn was inspiring.

"Girls," Molly called. "Come into the kitchen and have some tea."

She stared at Elizabeth and asked, "How old are you? You seem much older than Mary."

Mary glared at her mum.

"Nineteen."

Elizabeth laughed. "Sometimes age doesn't matter," she said.

"You know, Mary's twelve."

"She knows!"

"Do you have anything in common?"

"Science, fossils, extinction..." Mary answered.

"Making new discoveries," Elizabeth said. "There's nothing better than finding something old."

"It's what we do, Mum. Finding new old bones. Get it? It's new to us. That's a fossil joke."

"It's not a joke if you have to explain it," Molly said.

"I have one," Elizabeth said, "What do you call fossils that never move?"

"Lazy bones," Mary answered.

"Or my favorite," Elizabeth said, "How do you know if a fossil was afraid before it was petrified?"

"I love that one!"

"Oh, I see it now," Molly said, rolling her eyes. The girls cracked up.

They walked to the beach with Tray and spent most of the morning outdoors filling their baskets. Dark clouds formed overhead.

"We should go," Mary said to her friend. "I'll drop Tray off at home."

"Bring him," Elizabeth suggested. The dog would be more than welcome in her home.

They walked past Mary's house, climbed up the long hill where Elizabeth lived with her sisters, and reached Elizabeth's door as the sky opened up.

Happy to stay dry, Mary and Tray followed Elizabeth indoors. The cottage looked simple from the outside but was much bigger than Mary's house. The furniture was heavily carved. Velvet fabrics covered the chairs and sofa in the living room in various shades of green.

Mary marveled when she saw the library. Books lined three of the walls from floor to ceiling. The back wall contained a huge glass window, which filled the room with sunlight, and a double-glass door opened out onto a garden. Most visitors to the library admired the long decorative wooden table inlaid with marble rosettes and semiprecious stones. They glistened when the sun shone on them, but Mary placed them a distant second to the books on the shelves.

She spotted the newsletters spread out on the long table and eagerly pulled up a heavy wooden chair; upholstered in a jade-green velvet fabric, the seat made her think of her brother at his new job. The table sat at the center of the room and in the corner was an oversized desk shared by Elizabeth and her sisters. Newsletters from the London Geological Society, an inkwell, a jar of colorful sealing wax, gold-plated stamps, stationery, and plenty of drawing paper covered it.

"Look at all these books!" Mary exclaimed. "And I see you have newsletters from the London Geological Society going back a number of years up to the present. When we first met, you mentioned all of the discoveries recorded in the newsletters focus only on what men found. Is that true? Not one mention of women's or girls' contributions?"

"That's true. Even though they don't see us as experts, we can still learn from the information in these newsletters. Feel free to browse."

"Well, we'll have to prove them wrong."

"Are you hungry? We could go into the kitchen and get some food."

"And leave here? No, I never want to leave here."

"Let's get something to eat, and then you can explore."

What Mary really wanted to do was to look through every book in the library. Tray stayed by her side until Elizabeth filled a bowl with chopped chicken meat and placed it on the tiled kitchen floor for him. Tray licked the bowl clean.

"Where are your sisters?" Mary asked.

"Out getting supplies for the salve we make and sell."

"What does it do?"

"It soothes dry skin, stops itchiness, and heals minor wounds and rashes. It's made from plants. We grow the flowers in our garden for use in the salve, and sell it in the market in town."

"How do you know about salves?"

"Our library has an extensive collection on plants. My sister Margaret had a bad rash. Nothing got rid of it. So the three of us worked on coming up with something that did. The salve was soothing to her skin and within three days, her rash was gone. Here, take this."

"Thank you," Mary said. "My papa can use it. He's usually on the beach with me fossil-hunting when he's not working. And he sometimes has cuts on his hands from work."

"Sounds like you're close."

"We are. He's the reason I became interested in fossils. He reads a lot, but it's more than that. His imagination is big and you have to dream big to understand fossils. How about your sisters? Do they fossil-hunt? I've never seen them on the beach."

"They hunt for fossils on occasion when the weather's nice," Elizabeth answered, "but I'm the one who loves it. Like you, I'll go out even when the weather's bad. They won't. And I correspond with a few geologists from the London Geological Society. My brother's a lawyer. He introduced me to many of the scientists when we lived in London. After my parents died, he moved me and my sisters here. He knew we'd love being near the sea."

"I'm betting there are no women in the Society, right?"

"Not yet. It probably won't happen for a long time," Elizabeth said. "Changing the subject, it looks like you've finished your lunch. Did you like your salt cod casserole?"

"I did. I have never had anything like it."

"I know you're eager to get back to the library," Elizabeth said. "I have an idea."

She rummaged through the baskets, pulled out a few fossils, and placed them on a newspaper she spread across the desk. "I've been reading about these," Elizabeth said. "The London Geological Society says they're quite common and are found in many places throughout the world. I believe we have a lot of them in Lyme Regis."

"Here," she said, pointing to an article in the London Geological Society's newsletter, "it says Georges Curvier, head of the London Geological Society, believes fossils like these are millions of years old."

"Millions of years old!" Mary repeated, her brown eyes widening. "My papa taught me to close my eyes and try to imagine what these creatures looked like when they were alive. I see them swimming in the ocean or crawling on land. To hold something in our hands that's millions of years old is remarkable. I never tire of it.

"You're the only girl I've ever met who loves learning about fossils as much as I do," Mary continued. "So many people think I'm daft when I go on about them. Some even get mad at me because they think I'm lying; they think it's impossible anything would die out."

"Extinction's a hard concept for some," Elizabeth said. "I try to be patient with the nonbelievers. Somedays, I'm anything but. That's why I'm glad you're my friend."

Elizabeth picked up a fossil and held it to the light. "See the bluish-black color inside?"

"Yes. It looks like ink," Mary said.

"Precisely," Elizabeth answered. She went to the kitchen and came back with a glass of water and a thin paintbrush. Slowly she added a teaspoonful of water into the chamber of the fossil and swished it around with the paintbrush. The bluish-black substance loosened and took on a paste-like consistency. "Look, Mary. See. I think this is dried ink. They've been out of the water for so long that the ink hardened."

Elizabeth added a few more drops of water to get the right consistency. She then dabbed the soft end of the paintbrush into the chamber and swirled it around again, covering the rust-colored hairs of the brush completely with the blue-black ink.

"Do you paint?" Mary asked.

"Yes. I use my quill, or sometimes pastels to make images of my finds, which I send to the London Geological Society. Do you?"

"Yes. I learned watching my papa."

Elizabeth handed her friend a sheet of plain white paper and took one for herself. She gave Mary a different paintbrush.

They dabbed their paintbrushes into the liquid ink and painted pictures of the belemnite fossil, and as soon as all the ink was gone, Elizabeth added a few drops of water to the second fossil with the ink sac. "I'm sure we can find more on the beach," Elizabeth said. "We can collect them and use the ink to draw our finds. Mary, you should keep a record of your fossils. I'll be happy to send them to the London Geological Society for you. They collect this information because it's helpful."

Mary and Elizabeth talked while the ink on their drawings dried. Then she rolled up the picture of the belemnite fossil, said good-bye to her friend, and walked down the hill back to her house with Tray at her side.

CHAPTER 6

MARY GOT UP THE next morning and passed the front room, where her drawing hung in a frame Richard had made. Molly liked the idea of displaying her daughter's artwork. The drawing was so good that Molly thought she might be able to sell it and others once the shop officially opened.

Mary's parents were in an especially good mood; Richard had sold the chair.

"Your papa and I are going shopping. We're buying food with some of the money he made and paying some overdue bills. Old widow Beryl Powell is expecting last month's rent, too. What about your new friend, Elizabeth? When will you see her again?"

"She's with her family. I'll see her on Monday. And, Papa, I have something for you. Elizabeth gave me a salve to soothe the cuts on your hands. She and her sister make and sell them. She gave it to me as a gift, and I'm giving it to you."

Richard opened the tin, put a dab on the palm of his hands, and rubbed them together. It soothed his dry, chapped hands. ""Smells like lavender," he said. "Thank you, Mary."

Mary hugged her papa and mum good-bye and took Tray to the beach. Today, she carried two baskets. She'd fill them with as many belemnite fossils as she could carry. She loved the idea of reviving the ink to draw. Drawing was a close second to fossil-hunting. She picked up the craft early on by watching her father. Over time and with practice, her drawings improved.

Her father wanted to use the ink to make sketches of the furniture and cabinets for his customers.

These ink-filled creatures resembled decayed bullets, and today, the beach was full of them. As she moved away from the ocean, she came across a thick slab that had fallen from the cliffs. It was about the size of a small book. She flipped it over and found what looked like part of a large fish embedded within the rock. *What a treasure*, she thought.

Mary came home early with two baskets crammed with fossils; each one contained an ink sac. It didn't matter that she wasn't going to sell them. She had the book-shaped fish tail that would fetch a good price.

She placed the baskets next to a small wooden desk in her room. It was plain and more suited to Mary's taste than the ornate one in the library in Elizabeth's house. Her father had designed it for her. He had even carved her initials on the top of the desk and placed his underneath. Every time she sat at the desk, she stared at her initials and sometimes ran her fingers over the letters.

Outside, it started to rain. Something about today's storm troubled her.

Molly and Richard came home drenched. Molly tucked tea, flour, salt, and spices under her blouse, which kept them dry, and the wide rim around her bonnet kept a good portion of the rain off her face and the front of her blouse. The rain, however, had soaked through the top of her bonnet, making her dark-brown hair stick to her head, and the hem of her skirt and boots had gotten wet from the puddles.

Richard had left his hat at home and rain dripped from his hair into his eyes. His light-brown hair took on a darker color. He carried a half-pound of beef and a small wheel of cheese.

As soon as they got home, they put down their groceries and changed into dry clothing. Molly spent the rest of the day making supper, while Mary showed her papa all the new fossils. He took out a few paintbrushes, gave Mary a plain sheet of paper, and took one for himself. They sat together while Mary drew a picture of a belemnite fossil and Richard started one of Mary. It showed off her cheekbones and brown eyes.

"We must show this to Mum," Mary said.

"Do you really like it?"

"Yes, Papa."

"You know, if I have time tomorrow, I'm going to make easels for us," Richard said. "It would give us more space. With both of us drawing on your desk, it's tight."

"If we move the easels into the front room, we could display our drawings on them," Mary said. "It would make the room look pretty."

Molly added meat to the evening's supper and called her daughter downstairs to help as Joseph walked in from work. It was Saturday, so Mr. Stevens let his apprentices leave one hour early. Joseph walked about a mile from the textiles factory to his home in the rain. He had left his tools there so they would stay dry. It was warm outside, so he didn't shiver, but as soon as he entered his house, he took off his wet shoes, dried off, and changed into his nightgown.

***

DINNER AT THE ANNING household was exceptionally good that night, thanks to the meat in the porridge, and as a treat, Richard had persuaded Molly to purchase a tiny amount of cheese for dessert. Rich and creamy, it was a true extravagance in the Anning household.

Richard, Joseph, and Mary talked about sleeping in the next day and heading to the beach an hour or two later than usual. "I don't know if you'll get to the beach tomorrow," Molly said. "It hasn't stopped raining and the winds are fierce."

The rains continued. Thunder clapped and the room lit up from the lightning. This time, Richard was concerned. He looked out the window and noticed the ocean rising.

They lingered at the dinner table and continued to talk about their day and about plans for the new shop. Richard took the last piece of cheese and divided it into four equal chunks, making sure everyone got a piece. It was getting late and even though he was able to come home earlier than usual, Joseph excused himself and went to bed. Mary followed, with Tray behind her.

Molly and Richard stayed downstairs cleaning up. They talked about how proud they were of their children. Richard tried not to show he was on edge.

The raindrops came down heavy, hitting the window so hard that a few of the panes shook. Richard worried that the rotted wood framing some of the glass would break. It had happened once before and water had rushed inside. The fixes had been temporary.

This storm was a lot like the last big one, when they had crawled out of an upstairs bedroom to avoid drowning. That time, too, the rain had kept on coming.

***

"Wake up Mary and Joseph," Richard told Molly. "Get them down here to help. Now."

Groggy from sleep, Joseph pulled the covers back over his head, until a clap of thunder made him jump. Mary was awake. The deafening sounds of the thunder and the bright streaks of lightning filled her bedroom. Richard directed his children and Molly to move everything they could carry upstairs into the bedrooms and everything else into the kitchen. He closed the kitchen door and placed cloth bags filled with sand at the base to keep water from seeping under it and then stacked sandbags around the doorframe.

Richard lit a few candles. They flickered and interrupted the darkness between the lightning, which was the only good that came from the storm because it helped them see.

They worked quickly and in a few minutes, wood framing a pane of glass broke, and water poured into the front room. With a foot of water in the house, Richard directed Molly and his children upstairs. Mary had Tray with her and made sure he was safe in her bedroom.

Molly, Mary, Joseph, and Tray huddled close on Mary's bed while Richard tried his best to stop more rain and seawater from entering their home.

After another hour, the rain subsided. About two feet of water remained in the front room. Richard sloshed around and opened the front door; some of the water poured out. He called Molly and his children downstairs.

They grabbed brooms and swept the remaining water out the front door. The sun was beginning to rise. Instead of going to the seaside, they'd air out their home.

Richard and Joseph picked up the waterlogged bags, which dripped onto them and the floor. They placed the bags outside in the sun to dry.

The wooden floors in the front room desperately needed to air out. Molly and Mary scrubbed them to prevent mold from forming. By midday, they collapsed from fatigue.

Mary got up, warmed the leftover porridge, and set the kitchen table. They missed breakfast but didn't notice their hunger until they had put everything away.

Mary placed a clean rag on the floor and put Tray's food dish down. He ate scraps from their dinner.

Mary's stomach growled. She poured beer into everyone's glasses, dished out the food, and called her family in to eat. They ate in silence, too tired to talk.

Joseph almost missed lunch because he'd finally closed his eyes and gotten a few minutes of shut-eye. Glad it was Sunday, he planned to catch up on missed sleep. The flood combined with cleaning up after it, tired him out. After lunch, he retired to bed. "Don't wake me up for dinner," he said. "I need sleep more than food."

While Richard repaired the broken panes, he noticed Mary's troubled face. "Don't you worry, Mary," he said. "It'll be better than new. Maybe you can help me. Hand me my tools."

They spent the afternoon together fixing the window. Richard showed Mary how to restore the broken wooden frame and how to cut and securely place a piece of glass into the window. "See, my little thunderbolt," he said, "it's better than new."

Mary smiled, half-heartedly. Her house had flooded once before. She worried about the next time.

Molly marveled at how optimistic her husband was and believed the harder the situation, the more hopeful he became. It balanced their relationship. She handed him a cup of tea and went into the kitchen to put away the dishes.

Mary didn't say much while she helped her father.

"I know how much you hate storms, Mary," Richard said. "But you're stronger than any storm. Remember that."

Mary clenched her face at her father's remark. "I don't think I've told you about how much stronger you really are," he said. "It's why you're my little thunderbolt."

She looked up at him with sad, sleepy eyes.

"When you were a baby—just a year old—your mum, Joseph, and I went to a carnival in town. We were with friends. It was a glorious summer night, warm and clear."

"Oh, Papa, I love this story," Mary said. She started to smile.

"A caravan of performers came to Lyme Regis. Singers serenaded the crowds. A magician performed wondrous tricks. There were jugglers and a showman who trained horses to dance. I remember their hooves clomped and their tails flicked to keep the flies from biting them. We even had fireworks; they competed with the beauty of the starlit sky.

"The horses made a gentle high-pitched neigh. Then their neighs got louder. I thought the fireworks scared them, but after the fireworks stopped, they continued. It started as a song and became shrill. You could see fear in their eyes. Then the sky changed. The thunder was deafening, and then the lightning. It really was beautiful. Beautiful, until it struck you. Our family friend, Judith, was about to pick you up from your carriage and wrap you in a blanket. She briefly moved her hands away, and the lightning struck. Your body went completely limp. I plunged your entire limp body into a trowel of water used for the horses. I thought it would bring you 'round, and after one dozen tries, it did. Then, like magic, you became healthy. I swear you had been a sickly child. The lightning made you stronger. It's why you're my little thunderbolt."

"Oh Papa, you tell such good tales."

"Not this time. Ask your mum." Richard saw his daughter smile and it brightened his mood.

"Sure you're not fibbing?"

"No. Go ask your mum."

Molly always answered in the affirmative. It made her quiver each time she reflected back on that moment. Even though she wished it away, strangely enough, as Richard had said, Mary's frailty had disappeared after that incident.

CHAPTER 7

Tourist season began, and thanks to Elizabeth's letters to the London Geological Society, geologists Henry De la Beche, William Buckland, and William Conybeare requested a meeting with Mary.

"They want to meet me?" she asked.

"Yes, they've asked that you take them on a tour of the seaside. They also want to see your fossil collection and drawings," Elizabeth said.

"Do you think they'll listen?" Mary asked.

"Yes. This is your chance to show them what you know. I've told them about your finds. I've told them how smart you are. And it's not just me; some of the tourists who've met you and who've purchased fossils from you talk about the girl who knows so much about fossils."

"When are they coming?"

"At the end of August."

"Well, then, we need to study everything we know and don't know," Mary said. "I'll go through my lists of what I've recorded in my journal; I'll be ready for them."

Mary leafed through her journal and placed stars next to items she wanted to discuss.

***

Word spread about the unusual creatures found in the town of Lyme Regis. Tourists on holiday from London and other large cities mostly came for the saltwater spas and quiet. Once they arrived, they learned about the Annings' Fossil and Furniture

Shop. They spent their time on the beach, where they saw Mary collecting fossils. Many would question her about her finds, and she proudly shared her knowledge and told them about her family's shop. Business was so good, Richard spent more time fossil-hunting with his daughter than at his workshop. Tourists bought fossils, not furniture, and they showed them to their friends and family. More tourists arrived to see the strange creatures.

Joseph was there every Sunday. He divided his time between fossil-hunting with Mary and their papa and working in the shop to help his mum.

Supplies were getting low. Mary knew she had to find more fossils. She and her dad usually looked on the beach. Tourists looked there, too. It was getting too crowded for Richard. He decided to look elsewhere.

***

Joseph and Mary followed their father, as they did most Sundays. This time, instead of searching on the beach, he turned toward the cliffs. His children watched as he gradually placed his foot on top of a few of the protruding layers of limestone and shale to climb upward. If it wobbled, he'd move his foot to another stone.

His movements were deliberate and not rushed. Each time he stopped, he peered at the gaps between the layers in search of fossils. Every so often, it appeared as if a beige, rust, or black-colored fossil stared back at him. They stood out among the paler pieces of limestone and darker shades of shale.

Some of the pieces sat as if they were on a shelf waiting for someone to pluck them; others needed coaxing. He took his small hammer and carefully extracted a spiral-shaped ammonite complete with ridges. His children could tell each time he found something because he turned and smiled at them.

His pockets jingled as he climbed down. The first thing he said to his children was, "Don't tell Mum."

They knew Molly often said, "The higher the climb, the deeper the drop." Richard emptied his pockets and placed the ammonites in one of their baskets. "Want to join me?" he asked, as he climbed back up.

As he stood on one of the rocks, which jutted out, he bent down and offered his hand to his daughter. She accepted and he pulled her up about two feet off the ground. Joseph stepped back and watched. Not wanting to climb, he decided to hunt for fossils in the rocks at and below eye level. Tray stood by the muddy footsteps Mary left behind.

Mary and Richard left their baskets on the ground in order to keep their hands free. The tide was low and away from the base of the cliffs, so the water wouldn't wash their baskets out to sea. Mary draped a fabric sack over her shoulder; it had ample room to hold the fossils she discovered. Once the sack had been filled, she carefully placed one foot lower than the other, descending downward, and wished she had trousers on instead of a puffy dress.

Mary and Joseph promised their father they would "not tell Mum" about where they found these new ammonites. At home, they showed Molly their bounty. She admired the treasures and placed the speckled spiral seashells in the window to attract customers.

CHAPTER 8

RICHARD RETURNED TO THE cliffs alone. Something on his last trip had captured his attention. He had been more than midway to the top when he'd spotted it: a bony structure resembling a crocodile stuck between the rocks. Maybe the bone he'd found yesterday was part of it.

He wanted to tell Mary and wondered, *How would I tell Molly about this?*

He pulled himself up to get a better view. Before he put his full weight on a piece of shale or limestone, he tested it with the sole of his foot, tapping lightly and making sure it stayed in place.

Some of the rocks were wet from the ocean's spray and the previous night's rain. He pulled himself up higher, and as he reached for a rock resembling a small ledge, his hands slipped. He tumbled all the way down the cliff, hitting his head. When he reached the bottom, he stumbled again. Feeling dizzy, he tried to steady himself so that he could make his way home.

He lifted himself up again, took a few steps, and collapsed on the beach. A few tourists spotted him, and one of the locals who was out fishing ran to get a doctor. The physician who examined him saw he was still conscious. He sent someone to fetch Molly.

The boy who knocked on Molly's door told her to come quickly because her husband had a bad fall.

In a barely audible voice, Richard asked Molly to send for Mary and Joseph. She was afraid to leave him alone. The doctor waited while Molly walked as fast as she could up the hill to Elizabeth's house to get Mary.

Mary could tell something was wrong as soon as she saw her mum's face. She noticed her mother's eyes were red and her cheeks swollen from tears.

Molly told Mary her papa had fallen and they needed to get to the beach quickly. Elizabeth hugged her and said she'd send word to Joseph at Mr. Stevens's shop. Molly and Mary arrived first. Richard tried to talk.

"No matter, Papa," Mary said. "You don't have to say anything. We know you love us, and we love you."

As soon as he arrived, Joseph ran to his papa and held his hands. Tears filled his eyes as he felt him slip away. Molly gathered her children around her and held onto them tightly.

***

THE FAMILY HELD A small service for Richard. Mary placed three of her favorite ammonites inside her papa's coffin. She asked the funeral director for a lock of her father's hair. The next day, Mary, Joseph, and Molly walked to the ocean carrying a clump of Richard's thick brown hair wrapped in one of his handkerchiefs. She gave her mum and Joseph a few of the strands and kept some for herself. Together, they threw it into the waves. Then they each said their good-byes privately.

Family and friends gathered at the Anning household that afternoon. Elizabeth and her sisters were there, and so was Reverend Wheaton. Mr. Stevens closed the shop for a couple of hours and arrived at the Anning house with a few of the apprentices. He told Joseph to take the next few days off.

"Don't worry about work, Joseph," he said. "We can manage without you. You've lost your papa and need time to mourn. Come back on Monday and your job will be waiting for you."

He hugged the boy and offered his condolences to Molly. "If you need anything, you let me know. Joseph's a good boy."

Joseph thanked him and his friend James for coming. James, usually a talkative young man, didn't know what to say. They sat silently while Elizabeth and her sisters offered them a plate of food. Joseph declined. He wasn't hungry.

***

Over the next week, many of their neighbors brought food and waited on Molly, Joseph, and Mary. Richard's mother came to visit and talked to Molly about being strong. Molly spent most of her time in bed and frequently cried when she tried to speak.

Her mother-in-law stayed for the week. She was determined to coax Molly to eat. She helped Molly around the house and made sure her grandchildren were all right. She did her best to keep Molly steady and talked to her about finding some kind of work so they could keep their home. Mary overheard.

"I'll hunt for fossils," Mary told them. "We'll keep the shop open and sell as many fossils as I can find. Soon Joseph will be getting paid. Mr. Stevens will hire him in a couple of months. We'll be fine, Nana."

Mary believed they'd be all right, even though she missed her papa. Not having him around made her feel empty and sad. The guests who came by each day for the first few weeks after Richard's death were a distraction. They kept the Annings occupied.

Visits from friends and neighbors became less frequent and Richard's mother returned home to Colyton, which was seven miles away. Unpaved roads made the journey longer. The horse-drawn carriage took a roundabout route to get her home safely. Elizabeth was kind enough to hire a horse-drawn coach to bring her to and from the Annings' home. Molly, Joseph, and Mary would rely on one another, as they always did. Their house, however, was empty without Richard.

Joseph was the man of the house now. So much responsibility was a burden. To feel less troubled and with everyone gone, Joseph wanted to return to the cliffs. Mr. Stevens gave him a day off. He went into Mary's room and woke her up. "Let's go to the beach," he said.

He was still sad. Walking in his papa's footsteps would make him feel closer to him. He needed to know: What caused his father to climb so high?

CHAPTER 9

Tray followed Joseph and Mary as they walked down the hill to the ocean. He often ran along the shore, leaving paw prints in the sand. For Mary and Joseph, it was odd not having their father nearby.

"I'm not leaving here until I find what Papa was looking for," Joseph said.

"You're not going to climb the cliffs, are you?" Mary asked.

"You know I'd hate going up there—especially now. I don't want to fall. I want to see what Papa was after. He had to have spotted something to climb so high."

The two children studied the colors and shapes of the craggy cliff. Tray got between them and the rocks, and started barking.

"He's trying to tell us to stay back," Mary said. "He wants to keep us safe."

"Good dog," Joseph said.

"He saw Papa fall," Mary said. "Poor Tray. I think he misses him, too." She placed her basket down to pet Tray, and he leaned in against her.

Joseph brought his left hand up to his forehead to shield the sun from his eyes and squinted. It was brighter than usual. "What Papa was looking for had to be up high," Joseph said. "See anything?"

"No. Step back. We're too close."

"Makes sense," Joseph said. "The farther back we stand, the more we can see."

"You know, Joseph, I never really looked up. My eyes have always veered toward the ground, under the rocks, and at eye level on the cliffs."

Joseph and Mary covered almost every inch of the beach and peered hard at the cliffs, trying to leave no area uncovered. "I don't see anything," Mary said, "nothing at all." She sounded discouraged.

"I'm not giving up," Joseph said.

"Joseph, you know, this is going to sound strange, but I feel as if Papa is nearby. I don't see him, hear him, or feel him. I just sense him."

"You miss him like I do. I think he's a part of this beach. He's in our house, too, and everywhere on this island. We see his handiwork in everything he's made. It's as if bits and pieces of Papa washed into them, making them special. And here on the beach, when we look for fossils, we sense him nearby because it was Papa who taught us how to look for fossils. Most of all, he'll remain forever in our hearts."

Mary had never heard her brother speak so sweetly about their papa or about anyone. She could see his eyes filling with tears. She looked away because she knew her brother wouldn't want her to see him cry. She, too, tried her best not to cry as her throat ached. She was proud of her brother for feeling this way.

Joseph took a plain white handkerchief from his pocket, dabbed at his eyes, and wiped the sweat from his brow. It was midday and the sun was extremely warm. He inspected the cliffs again. Glare from the sun made it almost impossible to see. He squinted and looked again.

He moved slowly, covering large sections of the rocks with his gaze. Then he saw it. It was barely visible. A bony white creature was stuck between the limestone and shale high up on the cliffs.

"Mary! Mary!" he yelled. "Look! Do you see it?"

"What? Where?"

"There," Joseph pointed, yelling again.

A few tourists on the beach looked up from the sand to see where the noise came from. Some of them recognized the Anning children. Gossip spread quickly on the small island, and those in the crowd all knew these two young children were the ones who had lost their father.

Mary couldn't remember the last time she saw her brother so excited. He walked over to her, and from behind, placed his hands on his sister's shoulders slightly, turning her toward the creature in the cliffs. "Do you see it?" he asked.

"No. Not at all," she replied, feeling frustrated. "The sun is blinding."

"Look again." He tilted her head and moved her bonnet so it shielded the sun from her eyes. Finally, Mary spotted it.

It was extremely high up. *What was Papa thinking when he saw this?* "It's so long," Mary yelled, "and huge."

Joseph placed his hands over his sister's mouth. "Lower your voice. We don't want anyone else to spot it. It seems big."

"Big?" Mary said, "Nope, it's *huge* if we can see it all the way from down here. I'm sure it's even more enormous up close. We have to figure out how to free it."

"I have work tomorrow. I know you're coming back. You have to promise me you won't go climbing up after it by yourself. You hear me?"

Mary didn't answer. All she could think about was what it would look like up close and how she'd retrieve it in one piece. She wondered how she'd gather it without it breaking.

"Mary?" Joseph asked again. "I know you heard me. Promise me you won't go climbing those rocks. You hear? And make sure Tray doesn't follow you up there, either.'"

"Yes. Of course." Mary rarely lied. She didn't mean to. The pull of finding out what her papa found was strong. She knew she'd return.

"What do you think it is?" Joseph asked. "It's hard to tell from all the way down here. It looks a bit like a crocodile. I can almost make out the head. I don't see the rest of the body, though. I wonder what a crocodile was doing up there."

"I read in the London Geological Society's newsletter," Mary said, "that millions of years ago, most of this island was under water. It's why there are so many fossils here. Crocodiles were different back then. Some of them lived on land and ran around like dogs."

"Like Tray?"

"No, not like Tray, like wild dogs. They ran to escape predatory animals."

"With their rows of sharp teeth, it's hard to believe there were any creatures that would attack a crocodile," Joseph said.

"True, but there were. And other crocodiles lived in the ocean."

"Finding a crocodile, if it is a crocodile, would be astonishing, Mary. I wonder how much of it is in the rocks. It would be incredible if its entire body were up there."

"I know. We have to figure out how to unearth it. I wish Papa were here."

"I'll ask Mr. Stevens tomorrow. Maybe he can help us. For now, let's not tell anyone."

"What about Elizabeth? I trust her."

"I know. But let's keep this between us. We need to think about how we're going to remove this crocodile or whatever it is, in one piece."

"I don't know if I can keep this from her," Mary said. "She's my best friend and she may be able to help."

"Let's go home and make a plan."

Joseph had to pull his sister away from the cliffs. She kept turning her head over her shoulder, amazed at how this once-invisible creature stood out among the rocks. Tray trotted ahead and circled back to them because, every so often, Mary would stop walking and turn around. "Now that I can see it so clearly, I think everyone else can, too," she said.

Her brother smiled at her and took her arm in his hand to lead her home. "We'll talk about this at home," he said.

The tourists on the beach had returned to their digging. They gazed downward and pulled out fossils that were partially covered in the muddy saltwater.

"I'm glad they didn't see," Mary said.

"Me, too. It was impossible to spot, but now that we've located it, it's all I can see."

"We shouldn't tell Mum," Mary said.

"No. Not yet. Let's go home."

CHAPTER 10

WHILE MANY IN THE London Geological Society found it impossible to believe a twelve-year-old girl knew so much about fossils, the gossip about her continued. Tourists who traveled to Lyme Regis from London returned with stories about a spunky girl who seemed to be a fixture at the seaside. Mary made believers out of those who met her. She hoped she could do the same with the three men coming from the London Geological Society. If she could convince them, then maybe the head of the Society would listen to her. Maybe he'd even allow women to get credit for their finds and become members, too.

Mary hoped to unearth the relic trapped in the cliffs before the famed geologists arrived. She didn't want them taking credit for her father and Joseph's find. The newsletter from the London Geological Society, other scholarly papers, and books only mentioned finds by men. She and her brother had discussed it at length. They had to come up with a plan.

Joseph worked the entire week, and while he managed to do his work well, Mr. Stevens noticed his best apprentice was distracted. He knew Richard's passing was less than a month ago and that Joseph missed his papa. What he didn't know was all Joseph thought about was the crocodile in the cliffs.

Mary planned to visit Elizabeth but didn't know how to keep from telling her about the creature. Elizabeth knew her so well that if Mary had a secret, she'd be able to tell just by looking at her. Since she'd promised Joseph that she wouldn't tell anyone about the sighting, she avoided Elizabeth. She knew she had to convince Joseph that Elizabeth was an ally.

Mary and Tray walked to the beach. The sky was overcast and only two other people—tourists—were out hunting for fossils. She tried not to stare up at the rocks; she didn't want to call anyone's attention to the hiding creature, even the two people immersed in their diggings. They didn't seem to notice her, Tray, or the critter peeking back at her every time she glanced up.

Mary knew she had to bring home new fossils. Most of the finds in her family's shop had sold, and tourists kept coming by in search of new ones. Her mother requested she bring home as many as she could carry. Her mind, however, was up in the cliffs.

She looked up again and thought about climbing. *But how? It's so high. I could fall. And if I make it all the way up, how will I get back down? What if I tear my dress? Mum will know for sure. Joseph and I need help.*

She spotted two neighbors, a father and son, heading toward the ocean. They were carrying fishing poles. The man tipped his hat and smiled when he saw Mary.

As she gathered a few new curiosities and placed them in her basket, she decided she'd meet Joseph at Mr. Stevens's after work. This time, her discussion would be more of a persuasive argument to get Joseph to agree they needed to ask Mr. Stevens, Elizabeth, and others for help.

When her basket was full, she and Tray walked home. After washing the dirt from the fossils and polishing them as best as she could, she placed them in the display cases in the shop.

Then she told her mum she was going to stop by Mr. Stevens's to walk home with Joseph.

It pleased Molly that Mary wanted to spend time with her brother. She had no idea of her daughter's plan.

***

JOSEPH OFTEN WALKED HOME with James. Mary arrived early. She paced back and forth, becoming more and more impatient. Joseph and James should have been finished by now.

They were surprised to find her outside waiting. She made small talk about the new fossils she found on the beach and asked James if he liked working for Mr. Stevens. When he answered, Mary didn't listen. Her mind sped up. *When are we going to get to his house? I need to talk to my brother.*

James asked Mary a few questions. He repeated, "Have you found anything unusual on the beach?"

"Mary's head is still on the beach," Joseph answered for his sister. Then he gently kicked her without James seeing.

"Oh, I'm so sorry," Mary responded, and wondered, *Why did he ask if I found anything unusual? What does he know?*

"Um," Mary said. "I'm sorry again."

"I guess your mind is elsewhere," Joseph said.

***

AS SOON AS JAMES closed the door behind him and entered his house, Mary couldn't stop herself. She talked on and on about freeing the creature.

"Slow down," Joseph said.

"I'm excited."

"I see that, and so can everyone else." A few people heading home from work looked at Mary as if she was daft. She even overheard someone call her a hoddypeak.

"I'm not a hoddypeak," she yelled back.

"No. You're not a simpleton," Joseph said. "Never mind what others say. It's unlike you to care about that. More importantly, tell me again," Joseph said. "This time, say it sl-o-w-l-y."

Mary took a deep breath to calm down and was about to speed up again. Joseph could tell. He put his arm around his little sister's shoulders and smiled. "I'm glad to see you so happy. We haven't really smiled in a while."

"Okay, now tell me about your plan," he said.

"You might not like it," she said "because it involves getting help from Mr. Stevens and Elizabeth."

She didn't give her brother a chance to object. She launched into her argument. "Joseph, they've been so good to us. We have to trust them. Plus, you know we can't unearth that creature by ourselves.

"Tomorrow's Saturday and you get off early," Mary continued. "I'll meet you outside of Mr. Stevens's shop and then the two of us will go in to talk to him. We have some leftover wooden boards from Papa's old shop that we never got rid of. We can use them; we can make some sort of scaffolding to climb up the cliffs with it. If we place it against the rocks, it could keep us from falling."

"It's a good plan," Joseph said. "You're right. Climbing up the cliffs and retrieving the crocodile by ourselves can't be done. And there's no way we could carry it down. I'm sure it's too heavy. I know we have to ask others for help. Sometimes, it's hard. And, we have to be careful no one takes credit for our find."

"Maybe some of the apprentices can help, too. I'm sure Elizabeth will do whatever it takes to help us. We can even offer Mr. Stevens some money from the sale of the fossil once we sell it."

"He may do it for free," Joseph said. "He likes me. And he knows we don't have much money. It's a good idea, Mary. I have to learn to be more trusting, too. I want this to be *our* find."

"That's where Elizabeth can help us. She knows a few men at the London Geological Society. A few are coming here in about a month, and they can verify what this creature is. I think they'll be impressed with it. You know I am, even though we haven't seen it up close, yet. I can't stop thinking about it. It's even appearing in my dreams. I wonder what it is. I know it's something big, something unusual."

Once again, Mary couldn't stop chattering. Joseph looked at her and laughed. "It's a good plan. I'll ask Mr. Stevens tomorrow."

"And we must not share any of this with Mum," Joseph added. "You know it would upset her dearly if she knew we were going to climb up that cliff."

"I won't tell her," Mary said. "But she's sure to find out. Talk to Mr. Stevens first. If we tell Mum about the scaffolding and then show it to her, she'll see how safe it'll be. Then, maybe, she won't worry as much as she does."

"Mary, that's our mum you're talking about. She'll worry. When it comes to us, she worries."

"I know. But she'll come 'round."

CHAPTER 11

Mary arrived at Mr. Stevens's shop right after the apprentices left for the day. She marched right in to see Joseph and Mr. Stevens. Joseph had tipped him off so he wasn't surprised to see her.

"So, Miss Mary," Mr. Stevens said. "I hear you have a proposition for me."

"Yes, sir," Mary said. "Joseph and I want to talk to you about our project."

"Would you like a cup of tea?"

"No, thank you, sir."

"How about you?" Mr. Stevens looked at Joseph and poured himself a cup of tea.

"Yes, please." Joseph got a cup and poured some tea into it.

Mary was about to speak when Mr. Stevens interrupted, "I think you should have a cup of tea. Would you like some milk with it?"

Joseph laughed. Earlier in the day, when he'd told Mr. Stevens Mary was coming by to talk to him about their project, his boss asked Joseph to enlighten him.

"Your brother revealed all," he said.

"Then, can we count on you?" Mary asked, blowing gently on the hot cup of tea.

"You get right to the heart of the matter," Mr. Stevens said.

"That's my sister," Joseph said. "She's direct."

"I'd like to help you," Mr. Stevens said. "Joseph told me we can use some of the wood in your papa's shop. I have equipment, too. Maybe we can get a few of the apprentices to help. And Mary, Joseph told me neither of you has told your mum."

"Yes, that's right," Mary said.

"I won't go behind your mum's back. She's a good woman. I know she worries about the two of you. You'll have to tell her if you want my help. And, once the construction starts, she'll hear about it and she's sure to see it—unless you keep her indoors throughout the entire summer. "Do you think you can do that?" Mr. Stevens winked at her.

Mary smiled and shook her head. "When can we start?" she asked.

"Get your mum's permission and we'll start right away."

Mary grabbed Joseph's arm and pulled him up from his chair. "Let's go."

Mr. Stevens laughed. "A little patience, dear. Get your mum's approval and then we'll start on the scaffolding. How about tomorrow?"

"Can I come back later today with my mum's answer?"

"Yes. Let me know either way."

"I'll see you in a few minutes."

"Slow down. Why don't you tell your mum during supper and then the three of you can come back and talk to me. We can discuss it over a cup of tea."

"Thank you, Mr. Stevens. We'll be back after dinner."

Joseph quickened his pace to keep up with his little sister. "Didn't you hear Mr. Stevens tell you to slow down?" he asked.

"The sooner we get Mum's approval, the sooner Mr. Stevens will help."

"Yes, I know. And if we get Mum's permission tonight and she meets with Mr. Stevens, he's not going to start on the project in the dark. You have to give him a day or two."

"He said he'd start tomorrow."

"Can you slow down? I've never seen you walk so fast. I can't keep up with you."

"We're almost home, Joseph."

"I can see that," he said, breathing hard. "And you have to know building the scaffolding will take a bit of time, and we don't know what Mum will say. We need to think it through."

"We'll tell her Mr. Stevens will supervise. We'll tell her we won't climb on the cliffs like Papa did, that there'll be some kind of stairs supporting us. We'll tell her we aren't doing this alone."

"That's smart, Mary, but we should also tell her she can watch to make sure we'll be all right."

"I don't think she'd want to see us on the scaffolding. It'll scare her."

"Can you blame her?"

"No, but we'll be careful."

"I'm sure Papa was careful," Joseph said. "If you want Mum to give us permission, you have to emphasize Mr. Stevens will be in charge of everything."

Giving up control was hard for Mary. The idea of running the entire operation pleased her. She imagined herself directing and giving orders to everyone helping.

"And Mary, before you walk in the door, you need to be composed. Don't rush over to Mum and blurt everything out. You need to tell her calmly over dinner."

Mary didn't answer as she turned the doorknob to their house. Joseph put his hand on her arm and slowly pulled her back. "Mary, you know I want to find this creature as much as you do. Let's tell Mum together, and please be as calm as you can manage."

Mary went over to her mum, who was setting the table, and hugged her. Joseph filled three glasses with beer and placed them on the table. He dished the porridge into bowls, and with Mary's help, brought them to the table.

"Let's wait on Mum tonight," Mary said.

"What are you two up to?" Molly asked. "Is everything all right?"

"Yes, Mummy," Mary answered.

"Mary. What's going on? You never call me 'Mummy.' I can always tell when you're not telling me something."

"Mum," Joseph said, "Mary and I want to tell you something over dinner. We've given this a lot of thought."

"Ah, my sensible child, Joseph. You think things through. Mary's a lot like her papa. You're a dreamer like he was," Molly said, nodding toward Mary.

"I don't know about that, Mum," Mary said. "I can make plans and think things through."

"Yes, you can, dear girl, but you also dream. Like your papa, you dream big."

"Well, Mum, Joseph and I have a big dream we can easily accomplish with Mr. Stevens's help."

"Yes, that's what we want to tell you," Joseph said.

They started by telling Molly about their talk with Mr. Stevens and how he said he'd only help if he had her blessing. Molly liked that part best. She wasn't happy when they told her they believed Richard spotted something special in the cliffs and they hoped to find it, too. They emphasized over and over how safe it would be, thanks to the scaffolding. And Mary promised she'd let Mr. Stevens supervise.

After listening to their pleas, Molly became quiet for a few moments. The silence ate at Mary. Joseph shot her a look that said, *"Give Mum a few minutes to think."* She fidgeted in her chair and every so often looked up at her mum with imploring eyes.

Molly got up and put her dish and glass into the sink. "Mary and Joseph, let's clean up quickly. We don't want to keep Mr. Stevens waiting."

In her excitement, Mary jumped up and accidently kicked over her chair. It made a crashing sound. She ran over and hugged her mum. It was the first time since her papa's death that she saw her mum smile.

The three Annings took a leisurely stroll to Mr. Stevens's shop. Mary would have quickened their pace, but she knew better. Rushing her mum would not be smart. Instead, she slowed down and, every so often, skipped.

A cool breeze made the summer's night tolerable. By the time they reached their destination, a few stars were out. Mr. Stevens was glad to see Molly. He hadn't seen her since the funeral.

Surrounded by her children, Molly listened intently as Mr. Stevens told them how he planned to construct the scaffolding. He even took out a diagram to show her that he prepared after talking to Joseph. He promised to be there when Joseph and Mary climbed the ladder, which he'd secure in place. He gave his word he wouldn't let anything bad happen to his best apprentice or his little sister.

Molly gave her approval. Having Mr. Stevens oversee the project filled her with confidence.

Mr. Stevens told Mary and Joseph to meet him at the cliffs at 9 a.m. If it were left up to Mary, she'd have everyone at the beach even sooner at the crack of dawn, ready to go.

On the way home, Joseph and Mary walked along the cobble-stone streets talking about how they planned to capture the creature. Molly listened while her children urged her to come with them. She answered by saying, "I'll see how I feel in the morning."

The stars blanketed the sky. Mary gazed up and saw her first shooting star of the night. She let her mum and Joseph go inside ahead of her while she silently recited an old nursery rhyme her papa taught her: "Star light, star bright, the first star I see tonight; I wish I may, I wish I might, have the wish I wish tonight."

CHAPTER 12

Mary didn't need Tray to coax her out of bed. Joseph got up early, too. Molly had breakfast prepared on the table for her children and hugged them before they left. She wasn't ready to return to the area where Richard fell, so she would stay behind.

She made Mary promise to listen to Mr. Stevens, be patient, and climb only on the ladder and the scaffold, not the rocks. She also told Mary to make sure Tray stayed on the ground. She didn't have to tell Joseph any of this because she knew her son wouldn't do anything foolhardy.

"You know, Mum, you can come with us," Mary said.

"Yes. If you come, you can see how safe it'll be," Joseph said. "Are you sure you don't want to watch?"

"I'm not ready yet," she answered. "When you free the creature, then maybe I'll come. I'm still not sure how I'll feel being on the beach. You two, be careful."

"Mary, you should tell Elizabeth," Joseph said.

"I know, but I want to get to the beach."

"You have some time. I'll go to the beach to meet Mr. Stevens, and we'll wait for you."

Mary raced up the hill and knocked on Elizabeth's door. She took long, slow breaths and told Elizabeth a shortened version of her story. "Want to come?"

"Definitely!" Elizabeth told her sisters she was leaving, and she and Mary raced down the hill to the beach.

Mr. Stevens and a few of the apprentices were waiting for her at the base of the cliffs. He sent a number of apprentices and other volunteers to Mary's home to bring back more wood. They needed sturdy planks to walk across.

Joseph and a handful of volunteers emptied lumber and other equipment from a few horse-drawn carts.

With so many volunteers, construction could be completed in an afternoon. The scaffolding was almost five stories high. It didn't cover the entire cliff, just the area surrounding where the head peeked out.

Joseph pointed to the spot where the crocodile was hiding. It took Mr. Stevens and the others a while to locate it. It was easy to tell who spied the animal and who didn't by the smiles or looks of disappointment registered on their faces. James Mann scratched his head and kept on looking. Once he saw it, the eggshell-colored critter stood out among the rocks. A few others found it, too, but had to search for it again once they looked away.

As construction continued, more and more people in the village pitched in. A few men fishing put down their rods to lend a hand. By now, everyone in the small town of Lyme Regis knew Joseph and Mary had lost their father. They were happy to help. A number of the villagers had doubts about the creature but came to see the activity out of curiosity.

It was late in the day. Word about the crocodile spread fast. People passing by on their way from church or out for a walk gossiped about the project. Elizabeth's sisters headed over to the beach, too.

A crowd of 60 people gathered while Joseph, Mary, and Elizabeth climbed up a ladder secured to the scaffolding. Mary and Elizabeth picked up the hem of their skirts to avoid tripping. Joseph focused on freeing the crocodile.

He reached it before Mary did. His heart raced when he got an eye-to-eye view. The creature didn't look like the crocodiles in his books. Its head measured four feet in length and the empty eye socket was so round and large he could easily place his fist inside.

Some parts of the fossil had enough space around it for his hands to grasp. The trick was not to pull too hard; he didn't want to break it. The top of the head fit firmly into the rocks.

Mary's eyes widened when she came face to face with the creature. The size of it almost overwhelmed her. She whispered to her brother, "This is what Papa must have felt when he first saw it."

She turned to her best friend and saw the wonder on her face. "Isn't it glorious, Elizabeth? I've never seen anything like it. Never, ever."

"It truly is. And I don't know what it is either."

She handed her brother and Elizabeth a few of her papa's favorite tools: a small hammer and chisel that still worked. She'd had to sharpen the chisel prior to the climb; it was worn from too much use. Together, they dug around the head. Mr. Stevens, James, and a few volunteers used small hammers and shovels to free the creature. They listened to Mary as she emphasized that they move in an unhurried fashion, and she almost heard her father saying, "Small taps with the hammer. And gently pry the fossil from its enclosure. Moving too fast or using too much force can break the fossil. We do this so as not to damage the creature."

***

WHILE THE SCAFFOLD AND ladder went up quickly, Mary and Joseph knew freeing the head would take time. It was enormous. They could only see the head. They wondered if they'd find the body, too.

"This is magnificent," James said. "Mary, I now understand why you and Joseph love doing this. It's thrilling."

After working for several hours, they placed their hands on the skull and felt it loosen. It was ready to be freed. It would take several of them because it was so heavy. Slowly and carefully, they pulled the skull out of the cliffs and onto the scaffold.

Mr. Stevens instructed one of his apprentices to climb down the ladder and get some rope, which they tied to the creature's head. Mary made sure the rope was tight enough and the head secure.

He brought the pulley from his shop and used it to lower the head. One of the apprentices held the rope in place and slowly turned a lever to guide it down so it wouldn't swing against the rocks and break.

Joseph, Mary, Elizabeth, Mr. Stevens, James, and other volunteers descended the ladder. Once the head was on the ground, a crowd gathered around it.

"Look at those teeth," one person said. "There must be at least 100."

"200," Joseph said. He'd counted every one of them.

Mary doubted it was a crocodile because the snout was so narrow and the shape of the skull was different from pictures of crocodiles in her books.

Joseph explained how creatures change over time and this could, in fact, be a crocodile that was millions of years old. He wasn't sure. What they agreed on was the rest of the critter had to be nearby, and they were determined to find it.

Tray sniffed the creature's head and trotted around it while Mary, Joseph, Elizabeth, and a few of the other volunteers went back up the ladder to look for its body. Mr. Stevens had a few of his apprentices help load the heavy skull into his carriage to take it to the Annings' shop.

Before he left, he called Mary and Joseph to talk to him privately. "You'll look for it another time," he said. "It's past suppertime. I know your mother's worried about you. Let's be pleased with what we did today and not worry about tomorrow. I'm sure the two of you will find the rest of the creature. That's for another day."

Before leaving the beach for home, Elizabeth and Mary hugged good-bye. "See you tomorrow," Mary said. "I'm so glad you were here to help. Thank you."

"What an amazing discovery. You both should be so proud. I know your father would be."

Joseph hugged Elizabeth and thanked her. "I'll come by your shop tomorrow and help you clean and polish the creature," Elizabeth said. "In the meantime, I'm going home. It's late and I really want to look for clues in my library to see what it is. I'll let you know what I find."

Mr. Stevens promised Mary he'd keep the scaffolding in place so she could come back tomorrow when the sun would be out again. He didn't worry about Mary walking on it alone because it had held up under the weight of so many people.

Mary hugged Mr. Stevens and told him how grateful she was for his help. She thanked the other volunteers, too. Joseph was beaming, which made Mary happy. She was proud of her brother for being the one to discover this amazing beast.

They walked home together with Tray at their heels and talked about their father. "Elizabeth's right. Papa would have been so proud of us today," Mary said.

Mr. Stevens overheard her comment and said, "Yes. Today and every day."

***

THE CRITTER'S HEAD ARRIVED at the Annings' shop before Mary and Joseph got home. Mary was giddy. Joseph kept thinking about the creature's 200 teeth and his mind ran wild; he tried picturing what this crocodile looked like millions of years ago and imagined different bodies to fit the head. *Did it have scales like a snake? Maybe it had a long, pointy tail and short, stout feet. Or it could have had arms shaped like paddles for swimming in the ocean.* He was so deep in thought he didn't hear a word Mary said on their walk home.

They were excited to share the details of their day with their mum. When they got to the front door of their home, they paused because they could hear Molly inside singing. She hadn't sung since Richard had died. Her voice was sweet and she sang a popular folk song Richard often sang to their children. It was called, "My Poor Dog Tray."

When they walked in Molly was singing, "Poor dog, he was faithful and kind, to be sure; And he constantly loved me, although I was poor, and he licked me for kindness, my poor dog Tray."

Molly almost didn't notice them until Mary walked over and embraced her. "Oh, Mum, it's so good to hear you singing," she said. "I miss Papa's voice. He sang that song so beautifully. When I was little, he told me the songwriter wrote it for our Tray."

"And you believed him," Molly laughed.

"Yes. I believed everything Papa told me."

Tray curled up by Molly's feet while Mary and Joseph set the dinner table. "Mum, we have so much to tell you," Mary said.

"Yes, it was an exciting day," Joseph said. "What'd you think of the crocodile we captured?" Joseph knew his mum had seen the creature when it had been delivered.

"I'm proud of you," Molly said. "I don't think anyone's ever seen a creature that odd. It took the two of you to find it."

"Joseph and Papa deserve the credit," Mary said. "Joseph knew Papa had seen something special. He wouldn't let it go. And now it's here. We can inspect every inch of it."

"Mary's sure it's not a crocodile. I'm calling it that because I don't know what else to call it for now."

Mary and Joseph shared the day's details with Molly. They talked late into the evening. Joseph stretched, yawned, and headed to bed because he had to get up early the next morning for work. Mary hadn't realized how tired she was until she got up to clear the table.

As she passed through Joseph's bedroom to hers, he got up to talk to her. "Mary, promise me you'll stay safe while you look for the rest of the crocodile's body."

"It's not a crocodile, Joseph."

"Doesn't matter," Joseph said. "Whatever it is, please promise me you'll stay safe. I know you won't stop until you find it. Take Elizabeth with you. Swear to me you'll be careful."

"I promise."

She turned and walked into her bedroom with Tray at her side. Mary washed her face, put on her nightgown, and crawled under the floral quilt her mum had made. She couldn't stop thinking about what her life would be like if she found the rest of the fossil. *If I could find it and unearth it by myself, maybe the London Geological Society would accept girls. But I promised Joseph I'd ask for help. Why is it so hard for me to ask for help? I did it with the creature's head. If it weren't for Mr. Stevens, Elizabeth, and the others, the creature would still be lodged in the cliffs.*

I'll think about it tomorrow.

CHAPTER 13

THE FIRST THING MARY did when she woke up was to race to the front room to stare at the long-nosed specimen. It was remarkable. Joseph was at work.

This morning, Mary felt lighter and less anxious. Selling the fossil for a fair price would cover a few months' rent and food. Money aside, the thought of making a great scientific discovery delighted her. She even imagined seeing her name appear in the London Geological Society's newsletter.

Elizabeth stopped in while Mary ate her breakfast in the front room. She normally ate in the kitchen. However, she wanted to study every inch of the strange creature. She was careful not to spill jam on it.

Molly fixed Elizabeth a cup of tea and told the girls they'd probably be more comfortable sitting in the kitchen. They wouldn't hear of it. Molly understood their fascination with the colossal find.

It pleased Mary having Elizabeth's help. The fossil, encrusted with centuries of mud and layers of soil, needed someone with a gentle hand to restore it and ready it for sale. Removal took time. Mary knew Elizabeth would carefully clean and polish the head.

Visitors lined up outside. Word spread quickly, and everyone in town wanted to see the fossil.

"It's not ready for inspection," Mary said.

"You could let them in," Elizabeth said, "while we work on it."

"Yes," Molly came into the room. "I had the crew place it in the center of the room so they'd have to pass by the other items on sale."

"Let's let them in," Elizabeth said.

Mary opened the door and found a long line of people. A few inquired if the head was for sale. Mary told them no. She and Joseph had to convince Molly its value would triple once they found the creature's body. The skull was intact, with not a chip, crack, or dent. Elizabeth ran her fingers over the long snout. It was smooth on the outside, except for a few pieces of dirt, and the pointy teeth were still sharp. They worked on the head while the customers came by and asked questions.

Mary enjoyed the attention and was able to answer some of the questions. The one that stumped her and Elizabeth was the most popular one; everyone wanted to know: "What is it?"

Mary had a few guesses but wanted to be certain before she said anything.

The girls gently scrubbed the skull with rags and soapy water. Some of the dirty water flowed down the cabinet and onto the floor. Molly placed more rags on the floor to keep the water from spreading.

Once it was cleaned and polished, Elizabeth volunteered to spend the rest of the day helping Mary hunt for the body. Molly told them to go ahead and that she would take care of the shop. Mary was relieved to be outside. She hadn't minded the attention at first, but after a while, it had gotten a bit overwhelming. Going back to the beach with only a few people around was a better option than being surrounded by dozens in her shop.

"I see you're not fond of crowds," Elizabeth said.

"How could you tell?" Mary asked.

"I know you. You were getting quiet and it looked like you needed to be outside."

"I hope I wasn't rude."

"No, you weren't. It got hard to move around. There were so many people in your shop."

"Yes. It's never been that crowded."

"Mary, this is extraordinary. Everyone wants to see it. And now we need to find the rest of it."

"It's most likely near where we found the head, possibly somewhere in the cliffs," Mary said. "Joseph thinks it's below the head, but it could be above it, too. It's possible it got trapped in the cliffs and was decapitated. Let's start at the bottom and work our way up. We can search every crevice at and below eye level and go up from there. That way we won't have to climb in these impossible dresses. They're easy to trip over. I wish girls could wear pants. It would make fossil-hunting much easier."

Tray romped around the beach while Mary and Elizabeth examined almost every opening of the cliffs at eye level, with no luck. The sun was setting and they were getting hungry; they decided to come back the next day.

They spent a week in search of the body. On Sunday, Joseph joined them. They came home empty-handed.

Mary went to the beach on Monday by herself. Elizabeth was spending the day with her sisters, making salve. Mary had Tray to keep her company. She climbed the ladder attached to the scaffold and went higher than before. Every rock and crevice looked the same.

She ventured out the next day and left early because the weather changed. The rain pounded the rocks. She called Tray and they raced home. This time, she was the one who covered the windows on the first floor of her home with the wooden boards her papa had made. She was grateful that her papa had repaired the warped wood and broken panes in the front room, and showed her how to reinforce them.

The winds whooshed and trees shook in an angry sky. Molly worried about Joseph on his walk home. It was still early; maybe the rains would subside before quitting time.

A few large claps of thunder made Tray howl. He hid under Mary's bed when the thunder was so loud that it made the house rattle. Mary and Molly didn't like it, either.

Molly wanted Joseph to stay at Mr. Stevens's shop to avoid the rain. She worried about him catching a cold from the downpour. The rains continued and soaked Joseph down to his underclothes.

Molly lit a fire and Joseph changed into his nightshirt. They ate supper together and Joseph didn't need to ask his usual question, *"Did you find the crocodile's body?"* His sister's disappointment showed on her face. "Oh dear little sister who has absolutely no patience," he said. "You know this takes time."

Mary was about to protest when Joseph stopped her. "I'm confident you'll find it."

"If it continues like this, I won't."

Large drops hit the windows making pinging sounds. "I can't stand the rain," Mary said. "I wish it'd stop."

Fierce noises from the storm made it difficult to sleep. It wasn't just the violent rumbling thunder. The waves and heavy rains smashed into the rocks in the cliffs, which loosened them and caused them to plummet into the ocean. As each slab broke free from the cliffs, it made an explosive sound.

The storm finally subsided in the early morning hours, leaving an eerie calm. The sun came out. Joseph surveyed the exterior of the house before he left for work. Everything was in place. Inside, the house was dry.

The grounds were muddy, so Mary took Tray and headed over to Elizabeth's house. The streets were unusually quiet. Other than a few puddles and raindrops on some of the leaves, the sun was out working overtime.

***

Elizabeth had company. Henry De la Beche and William Conybeare arrived the night of the storm. They were delighted to meet Mary.

"We were just talking about you," Elizabeth said.

She introduced them to Mary. Henry De la Beche was fifteen, the same age as Joseph. His family lived in Lyme Regis; Mary remembered seeing him on the beach, fossil-hunting with his friends. They had never met because his family was in a higher social class. When he turned fourteen, his mother had sent him to Royal Military College. He was hoping to study geology because he loved fossil-hunting as much as Mary did and had plans to go to school to become a geologist.

William Conybeare was twelve years older than Mary; he worked as a geologist and was a founding member of the London Geological Society.

"All we've talked about is the fossil you've found," Henry said.

"That's what brought us here," William told her. "We were hoping to meet you, too, and look at the fossil you and your brother discovered."

"Joseph gets the credit," Mary said. "And he wouldn't have found it if it weren't for my papa."

"Yes, we've heard your father died. My condolences," Henry said.

"Mary's father spotted it first," Elizabeth said. "But it wouldn't have been found if it weren't for Mary and Joseph."

"The discovery took all of us," Mary said. "How'd you hear about it so quickly?"

"Elizabeth wrote us," William answered. "We'd like to visit your shop, which we've been hearing so much about. A few tourists who've purchased some of the fossils there told us about the girl on the beach who knows so much about science and fossils. We were planning on coming later this month, but we could not wait. We want to see this creature. I believe your brother thinks it's a crocodile."

"He's not sure," Mary said. "I believe it's something else."

"Any idea what?" Henry asked.

"Possibly. I can see why everyone thinks it's a crocodile. It resembles one. However, it also looks like a lizard. I'm not one hundred percent sure. I need to see the entire creature."

"Can you show us?" Henry asked.

"Yes."

"And we'd also like to see where you discovered it," William said. "Do you think the rest of its body is still somewhere inside the cliffs?"

"I'm not giving up," Mary answered. "Although, I'm beginning to have my doubts. I've combed almost every inch of the area. Nothing's turned up."

***

LATE IN THE AFTERNOON, the rain stopped and they headed to Mary's shop. Henry counted all of the teeth and William measured the head from the tip of the nostrils to the back of the skull. Mary noticed the awe on their faces. Nearsighted, Henry kept on taking off and putting on his wire-rimmed eyeglasses. At times, he got so close his nose rubbed up against the fossil.

William pulled out a small magnifying glass from his pocket. "Any chance you'd want to sell this now, Mary?"

"Not yet," she answered. "I promise to let you know as soon as I find the rest of it. Then we can talk. Until then, I can share this illustration I've made of it. You can show it to the others at the London Geological Society."

William and Henry planned to return to London the next day. Henry had school, and William needed to attend a meeting at the Society. They promised to tell the other geologists about their visit.

After they left, Mary and Tray walked to the beach. The prior night's storm caused a lot of damage. Mary held onto Tray's collar and made sure he stayed close by her side. She kept him from stumbling over the rocks that were strewn all over the areas they usually walked.

Big slabs of limestone and chunks of shale were scattered on the sand and mud. Some of the larger, thinner pieces had landed on top of smaller ones, making them teeter. Mud covered several rocks, and others looked as if the rain polished them. Mary had to take care not to slip.

The storm left a few presents. Pebble-sized ammonites were there for the taking. She turned over a medium-sized slab of rock and found a fish fossil embedded on the other side.

Mary spent so much time focused on the new creature, she hadn't done much collecting. Few fossils in her shop meant no income. Today's finds would sell; Mary knew customers would love these new curios.

She gathered as much as she could carry in her basket, looked up, and then dropped it. Everything in her basket scattered to the ground. She steadied her gaze upward. The body was in plain sight.

CHAPTER 14

Mary almost stumbled backward. It was a good thing Tray was there to steady her and keep her calm. Her excitement rose as she fixed her gaze on the creature. She refused to look away for fear it would vanish.

A few off-white colored bones showed themselves. It was a foot or two below the area where they found the skull. Its profile looked a bit like the skeleton of a crocodile, only longer—*maybe 10 or even 15 feet*, she guessed, then thought, *I need to get closer*.

Tray stood in front of her and barked, distracting her for a few seconds. "Oh, Tray," she said, "It's the rest of the body. It really is. I'm sure of it."

She picked up the fossils that had fallen, put them back in her basket, and placed it by the ladder fastened to the cliffs. She pulled hard on it, making sure it stayed intact and checked the scaffolding, first by tugging on it and then by putting one foot on it. It locked in place. As she climbed up the ladder, she carefully positioned her foot on the planks, testing each one with her weight. It was secure enough to hold all 90 pounds of her. She gave Tray a command to stay on the ground.

Once she got closer, she took out her hammer and chipped away at the rocks surrounding the creature's body. *This is amazing,* she almost said aloud. *Several of these bones must be at least three inches wide. And it's so long.*

She knew she'd have to call her team of volunteers to help her remove the body. This time, it would be a longer dig and she'd need more help because of the sheer size of the creature.

Mary was able to dig a bit with her hammer, freeing more of the fossil. However, the beast's ribs were stuck in the limestone. She carefully hammered away, revealing more of the animal's body.

She was so focused on the dig, she hadn't noticed the time. It was late and the sun was starting to set. She climbed down the ladder, picked up her basket, and gave Tray another hug. Together, they raced home.

Mary was out of breath when she reached her front door. Molly wasn't too concerned because Mary looked happy. Her cheeks had a rosy glow, and when she removed her bonnet, her brown hair stuck to her head damp from the sweat on her forehead.

Molly saw Mary's basket was full. She smiled as she told her daughter to slow down. "Take a few deep breaths and tell me what's made you so cheerful."

She was about to tell her mum about her day when Joseph turned the doorknob. He wasn't fully inside when Mary almost pounced. "Joseph!" her voice raised several octaves. "I found it. I found the creature's body."

"I knew you would," he laughed. "Can I come inside?"

"Sorry. I'm just a little excited."

"A little?" Molly laughed, pleased by her daughter's news. "Why don't we all sit down and then you can tell us everything."

"The thunderstorm helped," she said. "It washed away a few sections of the cliffs. Those loud thuds we heard last night were pieces of the cliff falling into the sea."

"I didn't think you'd be at the seaside today on account of the rain," Joseph interrupted.

"I wasn't until later," Mary said. "I spent the morning at Elizabeth's house. She introduced me to Henry De la Beche and William Conybeare. They're geologists—well, Mr. Conybeare is. Henry's hoping to be one someday soon. They came here to see the fossil you found."

"What did they think of the skull?"

"That it was amazing. They think it'll sell for a hefty price. And, they agree with me. It's not a crocodile."

"Then what is it?"

"They're not sure."

"Did you take them to the cliffs?"

"No. They wanted me to, but it was still raining and they had to get back to London. Soon after they left, the rain let up and I went to the beach."

"So they don't know about the body?"

"Nobody does. Well, except me, you, Mum, and Tray."

"That's good. I don't want them taking credit for your find. Mary, we need to keep this a secret. Someone else can visit the site and claim they found it first. You understand quite well that girls don't get credit for their finds. I'll ask Mr. Stevens for his help again; we'll have to reconstruct our team of volunteers."

"Joseph. It's so big. I think it's three times bigger than you or me."

The next day, Joseph asked Mr. Stevens for his help, and Mary went to tell Elizabeth the news. Elizabeth didn't invite Mary in; she grabbed her things and put on her shoes, and they headed out to the beach. Mary filled Elizabeth in on the way.

This time, Mary and Elizabeth had no trouble spotting the creature. Mary bunched up the hem of her dress with a belt around her waist and started climbing.

Elizabeth watched from the shore with Tray. She yelled to her friend, "I'm sure your mum hadn't seen it yet."

"Nope. You know her, all right. She'd have a fit if she knew how high it is, and worse, she'd be mad at me if she knew how high I climbed. I know she trusts me, but she'd feel much better knowing there were people helping. She thinks I saw it from the ground, which is true."

Some of the bottom part of the scaffold had blown away, making it impossible for Tray to jump on. Mary didn't want Tray up so high. She didn't think he was sure-footed, and she knew there was no way possible he'd climb the ladder. It swung a bit because only the top was secured to the cliffs.

Mary got closer and called to her friend. "You've got to come up and see this."

Elizabeth turned, told Tray to stay, and ascended the ladder. She watched as Mary climbed higher. She hesitated. She didn't have a deep fear of heights, but the creature was up higher than her comfort level allowed her to go. Her curiosity, however, was stronger than her fright.

"Don't look down, Elizabeth. I'll wait, and you can follow close behind."

"I was nervous the last time," Elizabeth said. "But with the excitement and all the people around, I tried not to think about it."

Mary placed her foot on the plank, testing it to make sure it was secure. She nodded, letting Elizabeth know it was safe to step on. As they got closer, Elizabeth marveled at the fossil's size.

"Look at this monster," Mary exclaimed.

They took out their small hammers and started to dig around it. Mary pointed out a number of the ribs caught in the rocks. Elizabeth didn't say much; she nodded, impressed by its massive size. Every so often, the silence was broken by high-pitched chirps and squawks coming from seagulls circling overhead.

"It sounds like they're saying, 'ha-ha-ha-ha,' " Elizabeth said.

"Yes," Mary answered. "Or maybe they're happy for us."

"I'm sure they are. Looking at this is hypnotic."

"It is. I could stay up here for a long, long time," Mary said. "I'm glad you're not afraid anymore."

"I've turned all of my attention to this monster. I know I will be a bit shaky coming down. Ascending is much easier than descending. I guess it's because I look down to see where I should put my foot. That scares me some. Yet, I am proud of us." The girls continued to dig for several hours, not noticing the afternoon fly by.

"It's getting late and the sun will be setting soon," Elizabeth said. "We didn't even stop for lunch. Are you all right?"

"Yes," Mary said, "we should be going home. I think we've dug as much as we could."

"We can work on it tomorrow," Elizabeth said. "I'll be here to help."

Each plank from the scaffolding formed a step. It was rickety in some places; that's why they gently placed a foot on each layer to test it.

Tray waited at the bottom of the ladder and wagged his tail as they got closer.

***

THE ANNINGS HAD DINNER at Elizabeth's house. Joseph told them Mr. Stevens agreed to help. "We can finally unite the head with the body," Joseph said. "We're a good team, little sister."

"Yes. We are. And we have to be grateful to our many friends."

***

THE NEXT MORNING, MR. Stevens and a crew of volunteers showed up for Mary and Joseph at the foot of the cliff. So many other people were there, too. Reverend Wheaton brought his congregation so they could see ancient creatures were real.

As Mary directed each volunteer, she heard her father's voice in her head telling her to move slowly and with caution. Her friends and neighbors gasped in awe as more of the creature was exposed. Mr. Stevens exclaimed, "Zounds," over and over again.

Mary worked hard. She chipped away at the rocks and discovered a backbone made up of sixty vertebrae. People on the ground placed bets; many still believed it was a crocodile. A few thought it was a fish, and others guessed it was an incredibly large lizard.

Mary understood why so many people said it was some kind of fish. Its tail looked like it belonged on a fish. Some people in town said it was part dolphin because it had flippers. She saw that, too. Others insisted it was a lizard because its upper body resembled the chests found on its smaller cousins. Mary thought it was an ichthyosaurus, part lizard and part fish. It resembled an image she'd seen in one of the books in Elizabeth's library.

Mr. Stevens brought lunch for the crew of volunteers. Joseph and Elizabeth practically had to pull Mary away from the fossil to eat. The midday sun was hot, and she needed a break. Mrs. Stevens handed out jam sandwiches and tea to the workers. Mary was going to gulp down her lunch, but Mr. and Mrs. Stevens asked her to spend time with them. She politely made some light conversation and as soon as she was finished, thanked them and headed back up the ladder.

If we keep going, she thought, *we'll be able to finish by dinner-time.*

As if he could read his sister's mind, Joseph stopped her from climbing and asked her to slow down. "If we don't finish today, we can come back next Sunday."

"Wait a whole week!"

"It's not going anywhere."

"He's right," Elizabeth said.

"I know, but..."

"Mary, we should be grateful to Mr. and Mrs. Stevens and everyone here who's helped," Joseph said.

Mr. Stevens overheard. He winked at Mary and called, "Let's get back to work. If we keep on going, we may be able to free most of this creature by dinnertime."

Mary smiled at Mr. Stevens. She'd give up sleep if it meant the creature would be in her shop by morning.

Many of the volunteers had trouble digging. In some areas, it was impossible separating bone from rock. Mary noticed and told everyone to change plans. Instead of digging out the creature bone by bone or trying to free it in one piece, they should dig under, above, and around the slabs of stone, forming a casing of sorts to protect it.

Each slab was between four and six feet long. Mary remembered her father telling her that sometimes it's better to take the rock with the creature still in it than trying to completely free it and risk having it break. She told Mr. Stevens, "We could have the volunteers lift it out on the attached slabs, which we could remove once it's on the ground."

"That's a smart idea, my girl."

At 6 p.m., the church bells rang. People stopped digging. Mary labored on. They were close. So close that Mr. Stevens asked everyone to stay a bit longer.

Seeing more of the critter up close gave the volunteers renewed energy. They agreed to continue onward for another hour or until the sun started to fade.

The stones around the creature loosened; it was time to fasten ropes around it and lower it to the ground. Mary knew it could smash into tiny pieces if it fell. She stopped again and told her crew to move slowly.

Several people held on tightly to the ropes lowering it to the ground. The wheels on the pulley turned slowly to avoid any friction between the wall of the cliffs and the fossil. Soon it was on the ground. Mr. Stevens measured it. Without the head, it was 17 feet long. No one had ever seen anything as strange as this before today. Those who helped worked in unison to haul it back to the Annings' shop.

***

MARY SPENT MONTHS REMOVING the stone and dirt, which clung to the bones. She was careful not to chip anything. She felt fortunate her father had left a workshop filled with useful tools.

It took most of a year, with occasional help from Joseph and Elizabeth. Once it was ready to be polished, she went into her papa's workshop and found an old cloth with his initials embroidered on it. She used the cloth to polish the fossil.

Throughout the year, Mr. Stevens inquired about the creature. He'd occasionally stop by to see the progress Mary had made. Visitors to the Annings' fossil shop also watched Mary as she meticulously worked on the fossil. Everyone remarked she was so patient. Her brother knew better. Thinking about how long it had taken Mary to prep the fossil made him smile. She had no choice but to be patient in that regard; if she rushed, she could damage her find.

***

JOSEPH LET MARY BREAK the news to Mr. Stevens when they were ready to sell it. Word spread quickly, and a long line of residents and tourists formed outside the door. They were there to see the polished part-fish, part-lizard monster.

Mary made several pictures of her find; she gave one to Elizabeth, who sent it off to Henry, and he showed it to William. After seeing the drawings, they met with Mary several times to see the creature and to follow her progress.

On their most recent visit, they brought William Buckland, another prominent geologist, to meet Mary. Molly put on a pot of tea and the men congregated around the creature. The head sat alongside the body because it took up most of the floor. Mary knew the head and body fit together. She wanted to connect the two pieces. However, the cramped front room left no space to display it as one long piece. Molly, Mary, and Joseph had to move the counters and chairs out of the front room to make room for it. They also had to limit the number of people entering the shop because of the cramped space.

The men marveled at the creature. William Buckland told Mary and Elizabeth it was called an "ichthyosaurus."

"I thought so," Mary said.

"Well, dear, you're correct."

"It's a Greek word meaning half fish, half lizard," William Buckland said. "It was from the Jurassic Period."

"So, it's more than 140 million years old?" Mary asked.

"Yes. That's correct," he answered.

He asked Mary for a drawing to show Georges Cuvier, a French naturalist, zoologist, and head of the London Geological Society. He, Henry, and William Conybeare assured her she'd get credit for finding the ichthyosaurus.

They wanted Mary to lend it to the London Geological Society, but knew Mary hoped to sell it. Henry Hoste Henley, a fossil collector who lived in a manor up the hill, offered to pay them 23 pounds. That would cover their outstanding bills, rent for two months, and enough food for the next six months.

Parting with the fossil would be hard for Mary. She admired looking at it. It made her think of her papa and her brother. This was a family effort, and her family needed the money. *Besides*, she thought, *it's taking up so much room.*

Mary made several drawings of the ichthyosaurus, capturing its long and pointy bird-like beak and large socket for the creature's eye. She placed them in old frames she found in her papa's shop and hung them on the walls so she could always look at them.

Even after it was sold and gone, visitors stopped by to meet the girl who discovered the half fish, half lizard. She enjoyed her celebrity status.

A MONTH AFTER THE sale, Mary read in the London Geological Society's newsletter that "Henry Hoste Henley found, unearthed, and sold the ichthyosaurus to the Museum of Natural Curiosities in London." It credited the museum for meticulously cleaning it and praised Henley for bringing it to the attention of the world.

She read the newsletter again, searching for her name. Molly noticed her daughter's frustration. "Let's go to Elizabeth's and talk to her about it," Molly said. "I'm sure she'll be able to sort it out. And I'm sure the three gentlemen who were here and who saw your find will come to your defense."

CHAPTER 15

ELIZABETH SAW THE DISAPPOINTMENT on Mary's face. "I read it, too," she said, opening the door to let her, Molly, and Tray inside. "I sent letters addressed to Henry and the two Williams explaining the oversight."

"Elizabeth," Mary said. "It wasn't an oversight. They didn't want to give credit to a twelve-year-old *girl*," emphasizing the word.

"Let's talk to them first," Elizabeth said.

"Mary's right," Molly said. "These gentlemen scholars think we're uneducated. And the fact that it was found by a girl well, it's a strike against her. And worse, Mary's only twelve, not an adult. That, too, makes a big difference. It's deliberate, not an oversight."

"They've met Mary and were impressed by how smart she is," Elizabeth said. "We need to be patient. I often forget how young Mary is when I'm with her."

"What are you thinking?" Mary asked, noticing her friend seemed to have something else on her mind.

"It could be Georges Cuvier," Elizabeth said. "He's not as open as the others. He may be behind this. After all, he's the one who approves all the stories that go in the newsletter."

"Did you send him a letter, too?" Mary asked.

"No. Not yet. He's not as receptive to me," Elizabeth said.

"Because you're a girl?" Mary asked.

"Possibly so," Elizabeth answered. "I'm waiting to talk to Henry and the two Williams. They know me and my family.

And they know you, too. You'd think men who'd believe these creatures, creatures that are millions of years old exist, would be more open minded.

"Let's focus on the positive," Elizabeth continued. "You're famous here. Most people in Lyme Regis don't read the London Geological Society's newsletter. And if they did, they'd know the article is wrong."

"True," Molly said. "Many of the people in town saw you unearth it. And those who didn't heard from others who did. Still, I feel slighted for my daughter."

***

ALMOST EVERY DAY, MARY asked Elizabeth if she had heard anything yet. The mail between Lyme Regis and London took about a week. Despite no word, the girls met daily on the beach and continued to look for more fossils. Mary's anger at the men at the London Geological Society didn't diminish her love of the search. While she didn't find anything quite as large as the ichthyosaurus, most days, she filled her basket with small ammonites and belemnites she knew she could sell.

Two weeks after Elizabeth sent out her letters, Henry came to visit at Elizabeth's house. Elizabeth had recently received replies from William Conybeare and William Buckland, promising to straighten out the error. Henry came in person because he knew Mary would be upset.

Mary was in her family's shop when Elizabeth and Henry arrived. Elizabeth handed Mary the two letters she received from the two Williams.

"You have to read these, Mary," Elizabeth said.

"Yes," said Henry. "You'll see, we'll meet with Georges Cuvier to discuss the oversight."

"Henry," Mary said. "It's much more than an oversight. I have hundreds of witnesses—people who helped me free the ichthyosaurus and those who have visited my shop. They know I discovered it. The men of the London Geological Society don't credit girls or women for their finds. It's hurtful and wrong."

"Yes. Elizabeth told me you'd say that," he said.

"She may be right," Elizabeth said.

"I am. Men don't give women—especially girls—credit," Mary said.

"True," Henry admitted. "But we saw your find. It was here in your shop. We are going to talk to Mr. Henley. Mary, I give you my word."

"I've heard he's been selling a lot of his fossils for hefty prices since taking credit for my find," Mary said. "I also heard he sold the ichthyosaurus for almost twice of what he paid me for it!"

"All true," Henry said. "But most everyone here in Lyme Regis saw you unearth it, and I'd guess that more than half the town has seen it in your shop. They know you're the one who found it. I'm sure we can sort this out."

"Has Mr. Cuvier seen it yet?" Mary asked.

"No," Henry answered. "I believe it's at the Museum of Natural Curiosities. Mary, we're going to talk to Mr. Cuvier. William Buckland and William Conybeare know him. As members of the Society, we'll fix this. I promise."

"And William Buckland is going to show Mr. Cuvier the illustration you made," Elizabeth said. "That should help."

"If you have more drawings, Mary, maybe of different angles of the ichthyosaurus, I'd like to take them with me back to London. It would show Mr. Cuvier the details of the creature."

Mary opened a drawer in the shop and took out several illustrations. She had detailed the creature's sides, back, front, tail, flippers, and head, and gave those renderings to Henry.

"I'll keep them safe and promise to return them to you," he said.

"Would you like to stay for a cup of tea?" she asked, softening.

"I would, but I want to get back to London. Mary, I promise to present your case to Mr. Cuvier and the members of the London Geological Society. And, Mary, Mr. Buckland, Mr. Conybeare, and I will speak on your behalf. We'll make sure you get credit for your find."

Despite the constant reassurances from Henry, Mary had her doubts. "Maybe he can come here and I can show him where I found it," Mary said.

"I'll see if I can arrange a meeting," Henry said.

CHAPTER 16

GEORGES JEAN-LÉOPOLD NICOLAS-FRÉDÉRIC CUVIER, better known as Georges, garnered great respect from the scientific community. His wrote a paper comparing living and fossilized elephants; it proved animals became extinct. Those who read his papers and listened to his lectures understood extinction wasn't a myth. He devoted most of his life to documenting the extinction of animals.

He welcomed William Buckland, William Conybeare, and Henry De la Beche into his office at the London Geological Society. The two Williams admired Georges. Henry had mixed feelings. On their way to the meeting they reminded Henry "to show some restraint."

Henry's anger showed. Both Williams offered to make the case for Mary in a calm manner. Henry decided to take a backseat until he was needed. He wasn't sure if he could keep quiet.

"I see you've come to speak on behalf of the girl," Georges said. "Umm, please excuse me. I forgot her name."

"Mary Anning," Henry said. His voice rose and the two Williams glared at him.

"I see you're fond of her, Henry," Georges said.

"Yes. I am."

"Sir," said William Buckland. "If you spend a little time listening to Miss Anning, you'd see how knowledgeable she is."

"Surely, you exaggerate," Georges said.

"No," said William Conybeare. "He's not, not at all. She's self-taught, well spoken, and you should see her with a hammer."

"She's to be admired," William Buckland said.

"I see Henry's not the only one here who's fond of Miss Anning."

"She's generous with her knowledge," William Buckland continued. "When I listened to her talk about the fossils she found, I learned a lot. You can learn from her, too."

"I doubt that," Georges said.

"The ichthyosaurus is on its way to the Museum of Natural Curiosities," Henry said. "You could see it there."

"Actually, it's not going to stay there long," Georges said.

"What do you mean?" Henry asked.

"It's on its way to the British Museum," Georges answered.

"What? When?" Henry asked.

"The owner of the Museum of Natural Curiosities sold it to the British Museum," Georges answered. "Once I verify it's real, everyone can see it. We're going to post an article in the Society's newsletter next week."

"It's real," Henry said.

"We've had forgeries in the past," Georges said.

"It's real," Henry repeated "And you need to credit Mary Anning. Here, let us show you the drawings she made of the ichthyosaurus."

He took out several illustrations. Each portrait showed a different angle of the creature. Georges looked at the pictures and noticed the intimate details. Every inch of the ichthyosaurus was meticulous—from its head to the tip of its tail.

"Did you see her draw these?" Georges asked.

"I did," Henry said. "She was at Elizabeth's house and I watched them create images of the ichthyosaurus. She's quite talented. And—more importantly—we saw the ichthyosaurus in her family's shop."

"It's difficult for me to believe a twelve-year old girl found this," Georges said pointing to one of the illustrations.

"She did," Henry said sounding annoyed.

"Don't feel dismayed, Henry," Georges said. "The ichthyosaurus should be here in a day or two. I promise you gentlemen I'll examine it as soon as it gets here."

"That's fine, William Buckland said. "And in the meantime, we'd like you to place a correction in the Society's newsletter stating the ichthyosaurus was discovered by Mary Anning. It should also say she sold it to Mr. Henley."

"He's been taking all the credit when all he did was purchase it from her," Henry said.

"I can't tell much from the drawings," Georges said.

"They're well detailed," William Conybeare said.

"Yes, they are," Georges said. "I need to see the real ichthyosaurus, not drawings of it. Then I can tell if it's authentic."

"It's authentic," Henry said.

"I'm sure you believe it is."

"Georges," William Buckland said, "We saw it, too. It's genuine."

"Gentlemen," Georges said. "I invite you to return once the ichthyosaurus is here at the museum. I'll give you my thoughts on it after I've examined it. In the meantime, I'm having a hard time believing a young girl found it."

"But sir," Henry said. "What if you come to Lyme Regis with us and meet Mary at her shop? She can take you on a tour of the cliffs and show you where she found the ichthyosaurus. You can also meet the many volunteers who helped her free the creature from the cliffs. And I know if you meet and speak with her, you'll be impressed with her depth of knowledge concerning fossils."

"I'm too busy," Georges said.

"How about we bring her to you?" William Buckland offered.

"That would be a waste of my time and your money," Georges answered.

"I see you're closed to the matter," Henry said.

"Be patient," Georges said. "I'll decide if I'll meet with her after I examine the ichthyosaurus. For now, I'm not convinced it's real. Do you gentlemen have any other business? If not, I should be getting back to work."

The three friends gathered their hats and coats and left the building.

"What a superior manner he has," Henry said.

"I don't know what we're going to tell Mary," William Buckland said.

"We'll tell her the truth," William Conybeare said.

"That he's a buffoon," Henry said.

"A well-educated one," William Buckland said. "He's highly respected."

"He needs better manners," Henry said.

"Henry, you know Mary best," William Conybeare said. "Can you tell her?"

"Yes," he sighed. "I'll return to Lyme Regis and talk to her."

"Tell her we'll fix this," William Buckland said.

***

HENRY TOOK THE NEXT ferry from Lyme Regis to London. The 151-mile trip took several hours. Mary was like a younger sister to him. Mr. Cuvier's stubbornness would upset her. He knew a hardship like this would not stop her from learning or moving forward. *That might be the secret behind her strength,* he thought. *Mary's one of the strongest people I have ever met.*

The ferry reached Lyme Regis at dinnertime. He'd stay at his mother's house for the night. She lived up the road from Elizabeth. He'd visit Mary in the morning. *There was no need to upset her,* he thought. *This news would most likely disturb her sleep. I'll stop by her shop after breakfast.*

***

HENRY PRACTICED HIS SPEECH to Mary in his head.

At her house, he came right out and told her about the meeting he and the two Williams had with Georges Cuvier.

"I appreciate your trying," Mary said, aiming not to sound angry.

"We did," Henry said. "William Conybeare and William Buckland made a case in your favor. Mr. Cuvier's so closed-minded and stubborn."

"I don't know him, but he seems like the type of person who doesn't like being told he's wrong," Mary said.

"Sounds like you've met him," Henry said. "It's going to take awhile. We need to wait until he's fully examined the ichthyosaurus."

"Would it help if I wrote to him?" Mary asked.

"I don't think so, but you could try," Henry answered.

"Will you take my letter to him?" Mary asked.

"Certainly, but I think he's annoyed with me."

"Why, what did you do?"

"I tried my best to stay calm, but my temper rose. Mary, he's infuriating."

"Well, thank you for standing up for me. I appreciate it."

"Glad to!" Henry said. "I have the day off. We could go to the beach. Let's take Tray."

"Before we go, I'd like to write that letter for you to take to Mr. Cuvier."

Her letter stated Joseph should get full credit for finding the head of the ichthyosaurus and she was responsible for finding, unearthing, and organizing a crew to free the body. She also mentioned her father was the first to spot it. Mary explained how the two pieces fit together and stated she had been fossil-hunting since she started walking. She didn't think the last part would impress Mr. Cuvier. She added it because it was true.

She listed a few of the names of the people in town who'd vouch for her, beginning with Mr. Stevens, Reverend Wheaton, and her best friend Elizabeth Philpot. She ended her letter inviting Mr. Cuvier to visit her in Lyme Regis, thinking if he met her, he'd see how much she knew about fossils.

She folded the letter, placed it into an envelope, and handed it to Henry. He promised he'd hand deliver it to Mr. Cuvier.

"Let's go to the beach," Henry said. "That'll get your mind off of this matter."

"True," she said, bending down to pet Tray, "being outdoors helps me forget about my troubles."

CHAPTER 17

A<small>N</small> <small>ENVELOPE</small> <small>APPEARED</small> <small>A</small> couple of weeks after Henry hand-delivered Mary's letter to Georges Cuvier. The return address was from the London Geological Society in London. Molly had picked up the mail. She was eager to open it and hoped it contained good news. She tried her best to be patient because it was addressed to "Miss Mary Anning," not her.

Mary was at her usual station—the beach. Molly planned to walk down there to give her daughter the envelope. Then she stopped herself. *What if it contains bad news? I'll delay this as long as possible. No need to upset my Mary.*

Joseph came home first. It was Saturday and Mr. Stevens always let his staff off early on Saturdays. Joseph saw the letter on the kitchen table.

"What's this?" he asked his mum.

"Looks like a reply from the London Geological Society for Mary."

"I'm surprised you didn't open it," he said.

"Yes. I'm eager to know what conclusions they've reached," Molly said. "I've heard this Mr. Cuvier isn't convinced the ichthyosaurus is real. I hope the news isn't disappointing."

Curiosity got the best of him. Joseph was about to open the letter when Mary walked in, with Tray trotting close behind. He handed the letter to Mary. She noticed the return address and ripped it right open. As she read it to herself, her mum saw Mary's brows furrow, forming crease lines on her forehead. Her mouth turned downward, too. Molly could tell the news wasn't good.

"It's from Mr. Cuvier. He doesn't believe the ichthyosaurus is real," Mary said.

"What does it say?" Molly asked.

"Why don't you take a few deep breaths and read it to us?" Joseph asked. He remained calm, which Mary appreciated.

Dear Miss Anning,

I need you to be patient. I have not seen the ichthyosaurus as of yet. My work has kept me busy and it was at the Museum of Natural Curiosities for a couple of weeks before it was sold to the British Museum. It's in storage, close to being unveiled for the public to see, and I repeat, you need to be patient. I will examine it in due time.

I must confess, despite testimonies from Henry De la Beche, William Buckland, and William Conybeare, I'm not convinced the ichthyosaurus is authentic. I have doubts a girl—I was told you are all of twelve years old—discovered, organized a party of volunteers to help unearth it, and meticulously cleaned and polished it.

Other than Mr. De la Beche, Mr. Buckland, and Mr. Conybeare, the other geologists in the Society whom I have discussed this with expressed their doubts, too.

You must admit it's odd someone so young could accomplish this feat; it's quite unheard of.

I was somewhat impressed by the drawings and wondered how someone so young could have such talent. I find it unlikely these were done by a twelve-year-old girl, even though Mr. De la Beche insisted that he saw you create a few of the drawings.

It's a serious charge you've made, stating you discovered the ichthyosaurus. This could undermine any credibility you may have among the people in your hometown. Mr. De la Beche said one of your first discoveries was a pterosaur skull, which you sold to a private collector. Since we have no proof of that, either, I can only say it's hearsay.

In regards to the ichthyosaurus, as I have said, I haven't seen the creature yet and you can see my case is strong. You will have to remain patient until I take the time to inspect it.

Sincerely,
Georges Cuvier
President of the London Geological Society

Mary didn't know whether to crumple the letter, rip it to shreds, or hold on to it to show Elizabeth and Henry. "I know so much about fossils and geology, possibly a lot more than many of the wealthy collectors and geologists who doubt me do," she said.

Joseph hugged his little sister while Molly put on the tea kettle. He paused for a while and finally said, "You need to keep this letter, Mary. Let's show it to Elizabeth, Henry, Mr. Buckland, and Mr. Conybeare. I'd like to show it to Mr. Stevens, too. He's a fair man. I'm sure he'll write his own letter to Mr. Cuvier, telling him about the lengths he went to—on both occasions—to first unearth the head and then the body."

The next morning Joseph went straight to Elizabeth's house, showed her the letter, and asked her to write to Mr. Cuvier. Then he showed the letter to Mr. Stevens. He noticed Mr. Stevens's hands tremble as he read the letter. His face flushed with anger, too. He didn't even ask how Mary felt; he knew, and said he'd write a letter to Mr. Cuvier stating how he took part in the dig while Mary supervised. He told Joseph to wait as he wrote it. He didn't want to put this off. Joseph left with Mr. Stevens's note.

CHAPTER 18

Mr. Cuvier's daughter, Clementine, came in carrying a stack of mail from Elizabeth Philpot, Elizabeth's brother, Mr. Stevens, Joseph, and Mary. Henry, William Buckland, and William Conybeare sent letters, too, as soon as they got word from Elizabeth.

Georges looked through the pile. He was annoyed the envelopes were addressed to his home, not to the Society.

"What's all this?" Clementine asked her father.

"Business," he answered, sounding disappointed.

"You love your work, Papa. But you look upset. What's wrong?"

Georges Cuvier explained why he thought little Mary Anning forged the ichthyosaurus's bones and had her friends write letters on her behalf. "You know, Clementine, Mary's the same age as you."

"Well then, you know how much I know about fossils," she said. "And you know I want to be a geologist someday—just like you."

"Yes, but I'm your teacher, Clementine, and you're a quick learner. Mary Anning doesn't have your background or your education."

"The only reason I'm a quick learner is because of my keen interest in the subject. If you try to teach someone with no interest, it is a lot harder for them to retain all this knowledge. Maybe it really is possible Mary Anning knows a lot about fossils and that she did discover this ichthyosaurus."

"Not you, too," he said.

"These letters make a convincing case," she said. "I read them while waiting for you. And you respect the geologists who wrote on Mary's behalf. Dad, just because she's a girl doesn't mean she didn't find it. What if it were me?"

He adored his daughter and knew he would not stand in the way of her becoming a geologist. In fact, he'd help her. He promised Clementine he'd examine the ichthyosaurus first thing the next day.

"How about now?" she asked. "I could come with you."

He had a hard time saying no to her. The two of them walked the five blocks to the British Museum. Everyone at the museum knew him and Clementine. She was a frequent visitor. It was one of her favorite places; she often accompanied him to the museum, and while her father worked, she spent hours looking at fossils.

***

GEORGES HAD NO TROUBLE getting access to the creature, which was still in storage. It took a dozen curators to carry the monster into the screening room. Several tools were available. Georges brought his own magnifying glass.

The men removed the ichthyosaurus from the large crate. Several sheets of paper covered it to keep it clean. Georges heard it was large; seeing it up close, however, surprised him.

"Papa, this is gigantic," Clementine said. "I had no idea it was this big. I can't wait to unwrap it. This is better than birthday presents."

The men who carried it in asked if he needed help with the wrapping. Seeing his daughter's smile, he said no. He knew she'd want to do the honors and it made it more special if they could do it together. He still had his doubts, but with his daughter by his side he hoped it was real.

The creature's snout peeked out from the wrapping. "Feel the sharpness of the teeth," Clementine said, running her hands gently over them and poking their pointy ends with her fingertips. She removed more of the paper and her brown eyes widened.

"Papa, I've never seen anything like it," she said. "And look at its tail. It *does* look like it came from a fish."

"What troubles me," he said, "is it's too unusual and too perfect." He took his magnifying glass out of his pocket and placed it on a nearby table.

"Papa, it's not possible a girl with no means could create something this fantastic."

"I'm surprised at you, Clementine," he said. "What'd you mean when you said 'a girl with no means could create something this fantastic?' I thought you believed girls could do anything."

"I *do* believe girls can do anything," she said. "What I meant is no one—not you or I—could fabricate something like this. It would take a lot of materials and money to make a forgery, and she doesn't have either."

"When did you get so smart?" he asked.

"Papa, does that mean you think it's authentic?"

"Not yet," he answered.

"I believe her," she said. "Just look at this." She stood back to admire the creature.

"And I've read most of those letters," she added. "I hope you don't mind, but I took a few with me. I read them while you were arranging for the men to bring the ichthyosaurus here. She has so many people defending her, people who witnessed the find. They have nothing to gain by not telling the truth about her."

"Clementine, if you don't become a geologist, you'd make a great lawyer," he said.

"No. I am going to be a geologist. I want to study these strange creatures. And other than social class, I'm a lot like Mary Anning. We both love hunting for fossils."

His daughter picked up the magnifying glass on the table and handed it to her father. "Let's examine this closely," she said.

"That's what I plan on doing, dear."

"How can you tell if it's a fake? It looks real to me."

"There's a series of questions I need answers to," he said.

"I know the answer to the first one," she said.

"What answer?"

"Where did it come from?"

"It's nice knowing you listen to me when I teach you about fossils," he said.

"We know it came from Lyme Regis," she said. "That's a fact. We have proof of it from the seller and from all of the people."

"Yes. That's true," he said. "I've also learned the ichthyosaurus lived in this region millions of years ago during the Jurassic Period."

"That's one for Mary!"

"I didn't know you were tallying points."

"I'm not," she said. "I'm rooting for her."

"Why take her side?"

"It's not about sides, Papa. It's about truth. I believe she's telling the truth. She gains nothing by lying."

"Well, you can tally another point for your friend," he said.

"Why?"

"While we said it's perfect, it's really not. There are no enhancements on it and there are a few small cracks on parts of the bones. I think if someone were to pass off a fake, they'd avoid the flaws.

"Also," he continued, "the head is separate from the body. They were found in the same area at two different times, and they fit together. It's a pair, all right."

"That makes three points for Mary!" Clementine said.

"I'm going to do the 'Lick test," he said. "Unless you want to do it."

"Blech. No thank you," she said, shaking her head. "Isn't that when you have to stick your tongue on the bone and see if it sticks to it?"

"Yes. *That's* it."

"What did you say?" Clementine said, laughing. "I couldn't understand you with your tongue stuck to the bone."

Wiping his mouth, he said, "There's more to it. Look at the inside of this bone, Clementine. It looks like a sponge with all those holes. That's the remains of its bone structure. Rocks don't have that. Since my tongue stuck to it, it makes it a bone, not a rock."

"Yes, another two points for Mary," she said.

"You mean one point."

"No, Papa, two—one for having your tongue stick to the bone and another for the spongy part you showed me. Two more points for Mary!"

"Glad to see you're so pleased," he said, tapping his fingers onto the bone.

"Now, what are you doing?" she asked.

"Listening for a hollow sound," he said. "You hear it when you tap your fingers on bone. Some bones are porous and others are solid. This has both."

"Victory is close," Clementine said, giggling. "Another two points for Mary. She has so many, Papa. I've lost track."

"And look here," Georges said, pointing to various parts of the bone. "Notice the colors. Overall, they are consistent. The teeth are lighter than the solid bones and there are darker colors on the porous ones."

"Papa?"

"Yes, Clementine."

"Can I come with you when you tell her?" she asked. "I want to see her face light up."

"What makes you think I'm going to tell her, and in person?"

"Papa, not only are you going to tell her, you're going to apologize to her," Clementine said. "All she wants is recognition. And you know it's what she deserves. Recognition from the head of the London Geological Society can help her work. More people will want to purchase fossils from a famous fossil hunter."

***

At the next meeting of the London Geological Society, Georges Cuvier apologized to Henry De la Beche, William Conybeare, and William Buckland in front of everyone. He told them he would place a correction in the Society's newsletter with an explanation of how he and his twelve-year-old daughter, Clementine, figured out Mary Annings' ichthyosaurus was authentic.

He then sent a letter to Mary Anning, apologizing for doubting her and for causing her grief. He told her he and his daughter,

Clementine, planned to visit Lyme Regis to meet with her and apologize in person.

After showing the letter to her mum and to Joseph, she shared it with Mr. Stevens and thanked him again for trusting her. She then ran all the way to Elizabeth's house to tell her the news. Henry was there visiting.

"I was going to stop by, Mary," he said. "I heard the good news. Mr. Cuvier apologized to me and the two Williams. He's also making corrections to run in the next newsletter."

Mary showed Henry and Elizabeth the letter Mr. Cuvier sent to her. They took turns hugging her.

"Feels good to be appreciated, doesn't it?" Elizabeth asked.

"Yes, yes, it does," she answered.

"Did you write back yet?" Henry asked.

"Yes," she answered. "I let Mr. Cuvier know I'd happily accept his apology."

"Glad to see you're not holding any grudges," Henry said.

"It's hard not to," Elizabeth said.

"True. It's a bit difficult. However, I'm so pleased," Mary said. "And it made Mum happy when I read it to her. I also shared it with Joseph and Mr. Stevens."

"Oh, and I want to send a note to the two Williams," she said. "I didn't forget about them. I'm lucky to have a lot of people rooting for me."

CHAPTER 19

MR. CUVIER AND CLEMENTINE took a late ferry from London and arrived in time for supper. They were staying at the hotel up on the hill. The ocean views from their rooms were magnificent.

With the sun out the next morning, they took advantage of the weather and strolled from their hotel to the Annings' Fossil and Furniture Shop. The sign Mary's papa had made still hung over the front door.

When he tipped his hat and asked about Mary, Molly knew it was Mr. Cuvier. He saw Molly's face tighten and knew she was not thrilled to see him. Clementine stepped forward, shook Molly's hand, and said, "My papa wants to apologize to Mary. And I think he wants to apologize to you, too. You're her mother, aren't you?"

"Yes. I am," Molly said. "I see your daughter has perfect manners."

"Yes, unlike her father," Mr. Cuvier said. "I'm sorry for causing you any hardships."

"Is Mary here?" Clementine asked.

"No. You'll find her on the beach near the cliffs," Molly said. "That's where she is most of the time."

Georges took Clementine's hand and they left the shop. The sun shone on Clementine's auburn hair; it brought out her red highlights. She had left her bonnet on the ferry. The intense heat didn't seem to bother her much. She looked forward to meeting Mary.

Georges acknowledged his mistakes when he made them and grew more confident walking hand-in-hand with his daughter. They walked down the road and turned the corner. Clementine let go of her father's hand as soon as she spotted Mary on the beach. She picked up the hem of her dress and ran over to her.

"Hello, I'm Clementine. Clementine Cuvier," she said.

Mary recognized her name and smiled. She put out her hand to shake Clementine's. Tray nudged in between them, wagging his tail. "I'm Mary Anning and this is my dog, Tray. He's friendly."

"That's my papa over there," she said. "He's come to apologize. I'm sorry for any hardships his stubbornness caused you."

"Thank you, Clementine."

"Will you show us where you found the ichthyosaurus?"

"Sure"

Georges Cuvier walked up to the girls. He tipped his hat and said, "Miss Anning, I apologize. I don't know what else to say, except I can be stubborn sometimes."

"Yes. I told her," Clementine said.

Mr. Cuvier blushed. "I hope you'll accept my apology."

"Considering you've come all this way to apologize, how can I not?" Mary asked.

"Well, Miss Anning, I'm sorry. We've made the corrections in the newsletter and Clementine and I would be grateful if you could show us where you found the ichthyosaurus."

"Papa," Clementine said, "Mary's agreed to give us a tour."

"And I accept your apology," she said.

"Thank you, Miss Anning."

"You may call me Mary."

Mary pointed to the top section of the cliffs where the head and the body once lived. She asked them to climb the ladder still attached to the rocks. The scaffold wasn't as full as on her last few visits. Each time she returned, which was daily, parts of the structure found its way into the ocean every time it rained.

Clementine climbed up a few rungs on the ladder. Mary told her if she looked in between the rocks, she might spot something from long ago peering back at her. "It's yours for the taking," she said.

Mary found a few belemnites and ammonites. She placed them in her basket and took out one of each. "Here. You can have these," she said handing them to Clementine. "I believe you know how to free the fossils from the rocks." "I do. I know a lot about fossils. We have that in common. We both love being outdoors searching for them. I just hate these big billowy dresses, though, they get in the way."

"Well, then," Mary said, "that's another thing we have in common. Girls who do this kind of work need to wear britches."

Clementine nodded in agreement. "Whenever we're fossil-hunting on a beach, my papa says I bring so much sand home with me that I could build my own island."

"Yes. I've been known to bring sand into my home, too," Mary said. "We should also look on the ground. The other day, I discovered what looked like gold-plated ammonites in the sand. They're fairly easy to spot because when the sun shines on them, they sparkle."

"I think you're talking about pyrite," Clementine said. "They lived in the sea about 150 million years ago and were cousins of squids and octopuses. The mineral pyrite, which gives it its sparkle, is also called fool's gold."

"Yes," said Mary. "The newsletter had an article about them."

"I'm glad you're still reading it."

"For a few seconds I thought I'd have nothing to do with the Society," Mary said. "But that would be daft."

"I find the information fascinating, too," Clementine said.

Mr. Cuvier listened to his daughter and her new friend talk about fossils. He also paid close attention while Mary spoke about her other finds in the area.

As she talked about her curios, the region, and the history of the area and its fossilized creatures, Mr. Cuvier could clearly recognize Mary's intelligence. *Everyone who's met her and told me about her was right,* he thought to himself. *She's well-spoken and quite knowledgeable. Plus, she has a hunger to learn. She's a lot like my Clementine.*

They walked toward the water. Something sticking partially out of the sand caught Mary's eye. It was gold-plated, coil-shaped, and fit perfectly into the palm of her hand.

"It's another piece of pyrite," Clementine said. "It would make a beautiful pendant."

"We can look for more," Mary said. "This beach is rich with fossils." She looked up and saw Mr. Cuvier wipe a drop of sweat from his forehead. "Or, you can come by my shop; my mum will make you a cup of tea and I can show you the other fossils I've found," she said. "And, I promised my friend, Elizabeth Philpot, that when you arrived, I'd invite her to meet you."

"I'd like that," Clementine said. "I met her once at the museum and I know her brother. He talks about her often."

Mr. Cuvier, Clementine, and Elizabeth had dinner at the Anning household. The food was simple and the discussions rich. Clementine asked Mary if she'd write to her. She found a friend who loved fossils as much as she did and wanted to keep in touch.

The Cuviers invited Mary to visit them in London. "When you come to London, Mary, we'll give you a tour of the city and of the British Museum," Mr. Cuvier said.

"Mary, the British Museum is my favorite place in the whole world," Clementine said. "I know you'd enjoy visiting it and seeing all of the different kinds of fossils. And if you come to visit, you can stay with us."

CHAPTER 20

MARY AND ELIZABETH SPENT the day on the beach with Tray. They talked about meeting Clementine and Mr. Cuvier. The two friends carried three baskets between them. One was filled with a picnic lunch and the other two were empty—but not for long.

That day, they spotted the usual small ammonites and belemnites. It didn't matter that they were common. The tiny trinkets pleased them. They could string them to make necklaces. They always sold in the Annings' shop—especially during tourist season.

Elizabeth looked at the collection in Mary's basket. "I don't see anything too unusual," she said. "Does it bother you?"

"No," Mary answered.

"After finding the ichthyosaurus, I'd expect you'd want to find another unique fossil, one that's large—very large."

"Of course, I do," Mary said, "And I'm sure I will. We still have a lot of uncovered territory here in Lyme Regis. And Elizabeth, it's the quest that keeps me going."

Mary turned over a small rock and brushed off the sand. She found something peeking back at her. "Come, look, Elizabeth. It's big and bulky, and I could use your help."

EPILOGUE

MARY'S LOVE OF FOSSIL-HUNTING continued throughout her life. In 1823, she unearthed her first complete *Plesiosaurus giganteus*. These large creatures were common in the Jurassic and first appeared in the Triassic Periods; that's more than 205 million years ago. Mary's find had an expansive flat body with a short tail and four long flippers for swimming.

Like penguins, the *Plesiosaurus giganteus* looked as if it flew underwater, thanks to its powerful flippers. The *Plesiosaurus* had an extremely long neck and small head. Other plesiosaurs had short necks with larger heads.

In 1828, Mary found the first British pterosaur, which dates back 200 million years. It measured slightly over three feet long and had a wingspan of five-and-a-half feet. Its teeth were large and pointy, good for tearing its prey. Geologists believed it walked on two legs, and when it landed, it folded its wings much like bats do today. Its long tail kept it balanced while it flew. The British Museum displayed the pterosaur in 1828 and labeled it "Flying Dragon."

The following year, she discovered a fossilized fish called *Squaloraja*, which looked like a cross between a shark and a ray. *Squaloraja* were bottom feeders from the Jurassic Period. They ate jellyfish and small squid and inhabited shallow waters.

In 1830, Mary found *Plesiosaurus macrocephalus*, which first appeared in the Triassic Period about 203 million years ago, and were common during the Jurassic Period. They were marine reptiles, not dinosaurs. The term *Plesiosaurus macro-*

cephalus translates to "near lizard." Their broad bodies had four long flippers, which made them soar through the ocean.

Despite Mary's major discoveries, many men in the London Geological Society ignored her because she was female. Mary's mother, Molly, however, encouraged her daughter and took pride in her many accomplishments. Molly was a good role model. She managed the money at home and ran the fossil shop. She was 78 when she died in 1842.

Mary's brother, Joseph, who worked as an upholsterer, continued to hunt for fossils in his spare time. He also helped his mother sell fossils in their shop. He married and had no surviving children. Joseph died in 1849. He was 53.

Mary died two years earlier, in 1847, from breast cancer. She was 47 years old. Toward the end of her life, Louis Agassiz, a naturalist, named two species of fossil fish after her—*Acrodus anningiae* and *Belonostomus anningiae*.

He also named a fossil fish species after Mary's good friend, Elizabeth Philpot. He called it *Eugnathus philpotae*.

Mary and Elizabeth remained close until Mary's death, and when geologists came to visit Mary, they also consulted with Elizabeth, who worked as a fossil collector, amateur geologist, and artist until her death in 1857.

Mary also stayed in touch with Henry De la Beche, William Conybeare, and William Buckland. They often visited Lyme Regis to see Mary, and she continued to give them and other prominent geologists tours of the region.

The three geologists collaborated on a number of scientific papers about their finds. Henry De la Beche became the first president of the Palaeontographical Society, established in 1847. Members of the Society devote their time to advancing knowledge of paleontology. The following year, in 1848, he was knighted for his contributions to the field of paleontology.

William Conybeare received the prestigious Wollaston Medal from the Geological Society. It's the highest honor one can receive for work as a geologist. He wrote *Outlines of the Geology of England and Wales* in 1822. This work greatly influenced the study of geology in Britain.

William Buckland was admired for his writings on a dinosaur fossil he named megalosaurus, which translates to "great lizard." Despite the "mega" part of its name, it measured about one-quarter of the size of the *T. rex*. Like a *Tyrannosaurus rex*, this great lizard was a carnivore from the Jurassic Period, and it walked on two legs.

Georges Cuvier, often called "The Father of Paleontology," was famous for establishing extinction as fact. He wrote in his essay, the "Theory of the Earth," published in 1813, that new species were created after periodic catastrophic floods.

His daughter, Clementine, died in her early twenties. Author John Angell James wrote a short memoir about her, called "The Flower Faded." It was published in 1838.

***

IN LIFE AND AFTER her death, Mary didn't receive a lot of attention for her work. Charles Dickens, author of many famous books and editor of *All the Year Round*, a weekly literary magazine, wrote an article about her. It ran in the February 1865 edition and covered the difficulties and triumphs of her life. The last line of the article read, "The carpenter's daughter has won a name for herself, and has deserved to win it."

The Geological Society, which did not allow women to join until 1904, noted her death in its annual presidential address.

Not too many know of Mary's accomplishments. That is changing. The Lyme Regis Museum, which houses a number of her finds, opened a Mary Anning wing. Staff at the museum lead fossil hunts and talk about Mary to visitors. Some of her fossils are also on display at the Natural History Museum in London.

Some people believe the famous tongue twister, "She Sells Seashells by the Seashore," was written about Mary Anning. Unfortunately, that's not true.

Mr. Stevens and James Mann are the only characters in this story who are not real.

The song "Poor Dog Tray" is from the National Library of Scotland (https://digital.nls.uk/english-ballads/archive/74895190?mode=transcription).

ACKNOWLEDGEMENTS

Writers sit in front of computers, working alone on their novels. The process works better when others are involved. My writer friends are amazing and generous with their time and advice. Carole Moore and Chelsea Lowe spent countless hours reading and rereading my rough drafts. Every writer needs a Carole Moore and Chelsea Lowe in their life!

Thanks to Bill Lee, my wonderful agent at the Lee-Steinberg Agency, for sending me an uplifting text about this book after reading it and for his determination in finding it a suitable home.

The Lyme Regis Museum's researchers were charitable with their time answering my emails about Mary and her family. The Museum has a Mary Anning wing, which according to its website, resides on the site of Mary's former home and fossil shop in Lyme Regis, Dorset, UK.

Also, many thanks to editors Claire Sielaff, Renee Rutledge, Shelona Belfon, and the team at Ulysses Press.

ABOUT THE AUTHOR

MICHELE C. HOLLOW WRITES about science, health, climate, pets, and wildlife for the *New York Times, AARP, Leaf Score, Inside the Animal Mind, Inside Your Cat's Mind, Inside Your Dog's Mind,* and other publications. She's also written a handful of books for middle grade students.

Printed in the USA
CPSIA information can be obtained
at www.ICGtesting.com
LVHW020804101024
793400LV00015B/318